A
Harlequin
Romance

OTHER

Harlequin Romances

by JOYCE DINGWELL

1179—WILL YOU SURRENDER
1229—A TASTE FOR LOVE
1251—VENICE AFFAIR
1296—THE WIND AND THE SPRAY
1320—SPANISH LACE
1342—THE FEEL OF SILK
1365—HOTEL SOUTHERLY
1401—ONE STRING FOR NURSE BOW
1426—GUARDIAN NURSE
1452—I AND MY HEART
1492—THE DRUMMER AND THE SONG
1517—CROWN OF FLOWERS
1541—CLOVE ORANGE
1566—SEPTEMBER STREET
1589—NICKEL WIFE
1615—A THOUSAND CANDLES
1633—RED GINGER BLOSSOM
1657—WIFE TO SIM
1688—THE POOL OF PINK LILIES
1738—THE MUTUAL LOOK
1772—SISTER PUSSYCAT
1808—THERE WERE THREE PRINCES

THE HABIT OF LOVE

by

JOYCE DINGWELL

HARLEQUIN BOOKS

TORONTO
WINNIPEG

Original hard cover edition published in 1974
by Mills & Boon Limited.

SBN 373-01826-6

Harlequin edition published November 1974

All the characters in this book have no existence outside the imagination of the Author, and have no relation whatsoever to anyone bearing the same name or names. They are not even distantly inspired by any individual known or unknown to the Author, and all the incidents are pure invention.

Printed in Canada

1826

CHAPTER ONE

'MIFMIF, ith nearly time!'

Small Helena was considered sophisticated enough by her proud parents to attend Brit's posture classes, but she was still young enough to be bothered by s's. Obviously, and Brit smiled ruefully and secretly as she superintended her weaving, wreathing line of girls, posture bothered her, too.

'Mifmif,' Helena began again, one eye on the wall clock which apparently she could read, because, noted Brit, it was nearly time.

'Yes, dear,' Brit conceded. 'One more sequence, class. The wind, girls, rustling through the leaves.'

They all loved this one, mainly, Brit suspected, because it was the last before their release, but she could be wrong there, for the wind entailed action, and all young things want action.

Brit looked round at the different winds. Plump Marcia, a good solid wind, one that would bang doors and scatter papers. Lenore, a delicate wind, scarcely a breeze, you could say. Jeanette——

'Time, Mifmif,' called Helena triumphantly, and the lesson was over. Out they ran, the St. Hilda day girls to their homes, the St. Hilda boarders to their school home. St. Hilda's posture class was finished for today.

How much had they absorbed? Brit shrugged as she gathered her things and prepared to leave too. It had worried her at first, since she was a born worrier, but Miss Asquith, the Head, had merely smiled.

'My dear, their parents do not ask results, all they

want is for their child to be availed everything that offers. Speak to Miss Pidcock' ... Miss Pidcock was the music mistress ... 'and she'll tell you that quite often a girl doesn't turn up for her lesson at all, but so long as Miss Pidcock can drum *Moon Moths* into them, or *Winter Sleighride,* the parents are content. We are strictly a social school, so salve your conscience.'

Brit had salved it, but she never had succeeded in really enjoying her post apart from the fact that it paid satisfactory money. She would have liked to have achieved results. She was fond of children, and wanted to teach them something, not just provide another social extra. But posture to preparatory girls was premature, she strongly suspected; sixes to twelves needed unhindered action, not discipline and restraint. Still, it paid money. And money was what they ... *Cara* ... must have.

It was half dark by the time Brit finished her daily school report and left northside St. Hilda's behind her. When she reached their western suburban flat it would be night. She wished for once, *if just for once,* that Cara would put on their outside light. On winter evenings like this you looked for a light. But Cara would be curled up by the electric fire, painting her fingernails, or her toes, or forgetting, as ever, to start their evening meal. Then if Brit said anything to her about the light, she would retort, and rightly: 'But you always go on about money, Brittie.'

Brit was aware she often did. She was well paid, but the pay had to stretch for two, it had to include Cara. Cara was at ballet school, an expensive, exclusive school. One day, Cara always promised, everything would be repaid, but until she was ready, or until someone discovered her ...

Besides ... with a sweet little Cara smile ... remember how Mummy and Daddy had believed in giving her a chance.

Giving Cara a chance. If Brit had wanted to forget that, certainly Cara would not have given Brit the chance. Not that Brit did want to forget. She was as blindly proud and as blindly devoted to her younger sister as her parents had been to their baby daughter.

Brit had been a disappointment to her parents, she had known that from the age of six. A much wiser six than Helena, Brit thought now, buttoning her coat collar from Sydney's sharp August wind. She could remember it all as clearly as though it had been said last week, not all those years ago.

'Willis' ... Willis had been her father ... 'you're wasting your time on this one,' Mother had said.

Her father had sighed and agreed: 'Yes, Edith.' Edith was Mother. 'I did hope you might pass on your gift.'

Brit had known what the 'gift' was. Her mother had been a dancer. She had married Willis Smith after his successful *Hinterland* ballet, a music sequence that had swept all the Australian states but still never graduated from Australia; also a success Willis Smith had never repeated. He was working on one then, he was always working on one, but how, he had said irascibly to his wife, could he hope to achieve anything with no one to help him? For Edith had lost her gift with maternity and his daughter Brit obviously had no gift. The child moved nicely, stood well, but there was nothing else there. Willis Smith had said all that to his wife, and small Brit had heard.

She had stood listening at the other side of the door. Then she had listened to her mother telling her father there would be another baby, and because he was so pleased about it, about what it might mean, Brit had been pleased, too, had loved the baby even before it arrived.

And when Cara had arrived she had adored her. It had not needed her parents' frequent injunctions later, when Cara had shown definite talent right from an infant, to do everything humanly possible to give Cara her chance.

Only . . . and Brit stepped into the appropriate bus ... the chance seemed to be taking a long time. Brit was twenty-five now. Cara was nineteen. A lovely butterfly of a nineteen, not, as her father had said quite fondly of his elder girl, a brown moth.

'You're our little brown moth.' He had patted Brit's head.

Sometimes Brit had felt like protesting. Around twenty-two she had definitely felt like that, for twenty-two is dreaming time, time for bright wings and long flight. Certainly no brown moth phase. But her mother had died, and she could see how bereft her father was. Also, her father's sister had come to live with them, and Aunt Truda had supported her brother in his beliefs. Once Brit remembered Aunt Truda saying loudly and with asperity: 'There's only room in a family for one shining light.' She had meant it, of course, against *her*, Brit had miserably deduced. She remembered, too, how she had shrunk sensitively away.

Then father had died. Then, several months ago now, Aunt Truda.

'I suppose,' Cara had said faintly when the family income had been diminished to only one earning, 'I'd better do something.' She had looked appealingly at Brit, and when Cara did that ...

'You have to finish first, darling,' Brit had assured her. 'You have to have your chance.'

Giving Cara her chance.

The bus was approaching the stop nearest to the flat. Brit pulled the cord and got out. It was only a hundred yards to the apartment, but every step of the way she thought eagerly: If only the light is on saying 'Come in. You're home.' She would have loved a welcoming light. If only Cara had started dinner.

Then she reached Lockwood Court and her heart ascended. John's car was in the parking yard. So John was visiting them. Why, it was as good as a light, Brit thought gladly, definitely better than chops being grilled.

She was actually singing as she ran up the stairs.

Cara was toasting herself, as Brit had expected, but because John was there she was not finger or toe-painting. Instead she was looking over some ballet music he had brought across. John Ferris was following the same road Willis Smith had, though so far he had gained not even one success. Still, he was young, only a little older than Brit. Brit glanced at the sheets that Cara studied and saw that John had progressed with them since last time. That was good. She smiled across at the tall, fair young man.

He smiled back ... and Brit, being a woman, even though a rather naïve one, knew there was something special in that smile. Also that it was for her. She was glad, because she felt something rather special for John.

A little irritably as she watched the quick exchange, Cara complained: 'Must have been an easy day for you, Brit, you seem fresh as a daisy. Oh, lord, have I had a grind and a bore!'

Brit looked at her sister with loving sympathy. That glance from John helped her do it, because, she thought, I can well afford it. In John, I am ... and will be? ... rich.

'Stopping for dinner?' she asked the man.

'Will it stretch that far?' he grinned.
'If Cara will halve her chop.'
'Why me? I've been on my toes for hours.'
And I have been, thought Brit, on my feet, on my senses, on my discretion, tact and best behaviour (for social St. Hilda's demanded that) all day.
'I was joking, of course,' she said. 'There's plenty.'
There wasn't, but Brit ate at school, so she didn't need two hot meals.
Over the dinner, John explained his new sequence. He was calling his ballet *Southern Cross*. Cara got up and did some spontaneous interpretation for him. She kicked off her shoes and took up a scarf, but that was the extent of her props, and it was enough. She had definite talent.
There was silence as she twisted and wreathed. She was moonlight seeking the stars of the cross, thought Brit, and she looked a little secretly to see if John, too, was feeling that.
He obviously did feel it. He was enrapt. But, evidently sensing her glance, he looked at Brit, and his eyes were warm ... *and for her*.
'It has to be Europe,' John said later as he rolled up the music. 'There's nothing offering here.'
'I feel that, too,' Cara came in plaintively.
'But, darling,' remonstrated Brit, 'but, Cara, it has to be here for you. I mean—well, it just has to be, and you know it.' She said it a little anxiously. One never knew with Cara.
'I could go,' pouted her younger sister. 'Other girls go. Live in a garret, all that.' But she said it vaguely, without conviction. She had no conviction, and neither had Brit. Cara would starve in an attic, Brit knew, unless, as was quite likely, someone saw her (for you had only to see her) and came to her rescue.

'Ballet is improving here,' Brit offered a little weakly.

'Improvement!' disparaged Cara.

'I feel it will arrive in a grand manner,' came in John, 'and quite soon. But with my own line of goods I have to be on the initial rung. So I must try Europe first.' He got up. 'Thanks for the meal, Brit, thanks for the listening ear.'

'Thanking me for the dancing feet?' put in Cara.

'You know I always do that,' John smiled, but it was not the smile he gave Brit, and Cara knew that.

When he had gone Cara said pettishly: 'His ballet is no good.'

'I thought it had promise.'

'But you wouldn't know, would you?'

'Not like you, darling,' placated Brit. She knew that Cara, lovely, spoiled Cara, had seen those personal looks, so she felt she could forgive her resentment.

Cara was regarding her sister speculatively. Always she had rejoiced in being the family glittering light, but wasn't there something quietly attractive, *enduringly* attractive, in Brit's less than prettiness? Brit ... sweet Maiden in Greek ... and that indubitably was Brit. Sweet. Cara stirred a little impatiently. Some men found sweetness more attractive than beauty. Obviously John had. She had seen his glowing eyes, a glow for her sister.

She stared at Brit covertly. Once she had been pleased at her own suave maturity, even at six years the junior, over her sister. She had been more polished, more sophisticated, she knew, more the finished article. Now Brit's youngness ... young at near twenty-six! ... vaguely irritated her. Why, she looked almost girlish.

'Some of your pupils have rubbed off on you,' she said a little spitefully.

'Then I hope it's not Helena,' giggled Brit. She added: 'She calls me Mifmif.'

'How do you stand the little pigs?'

'They're not really, they're just not ready for moods and what-have-yous yet. Still, I don't mind admitting I'm not that keen, either, but——'

'But it's good money.' Cara came in quickly with that. She didn't want Brit to descend the financial ladder by changing to some less lucrative job.

Finance reminded her of something.

'Mail,' she said. 'Two bills, by the windowpane envelopes. Money, money. What a pest it is!'

Brit nodded, and sighed slightly. She took up the letters and opened the first. A bill, as Cara had said. Then, a little absently, she opened the next letter.

It was from a firm of solicitors called ... but that didn't matter. What they said was what mattered. Most of all what they enclosed.

They enclosed a letter from the girl's aunt. Dead Aunt Truda. But the letter was for one girl only—for Brit.

'My dear Brit' ... how strange, how moving, thought Brit, to read a letter written by a hand that would write no more ... 'By the time this is received by you I shall have left you. I have given strict orders to my solicitors that on no account are you to receive this until I have gone, and until all my concerns have been wound up.' —Concerns? Aunt Truda? But Aunt Truda had been poor; she had had to come to them because of that, because living by yourself was too expensive. Perhaps, though, the old lady had been sentimental over some trinkets she possessed, for Brit felt sure she would have possessed no more than that. Probably a print, or an ornament. Some such.

'I was not what you could have called a wealthy woman; Brit, but I was far more comfortable than your father thought. I started with a little but had the good fortune of excellent help and profitable advice. However, I kept it to myself. Unkind of me, I suppose, not to have helped Willis more, but I did pay my way and helping my brother only meant helping someone else, and frankly, Brit, that someone else has had more than her share of help. *You* have had nothing.'

... I, Aunt Truda? But you yourself once said, and said it with firmness, with asperity: 'There's only room in a family for one shining light.' Didn't you mean that there was only room for Cara, that everything should be for Cara? You couldn't have meant——

'Cara,' continued the rather spidery writing, 'can and should be able to look after herself. She has talent, and certainly nothing has been spared to encourage that talent.

'But everything was spared when it came to you, and that is why I am writing this now. I have left a bequest with my lawyers to pay you the sum of——'

Brit read that sum again. Read it a third time.

'I would like to make a stipulation as to how you deal with this money. but my solicitors tell me that at your responsible age this is not advised.

'But I can suggest, and the solicitors agree with me, that an annuity would be a good thing.

'However, I do see that trying to control other lives, young lives, is not an old lady's prerogative, so I leave you this money as a gift. You are absolutely free to do what you like with it.

'By the time you read this all death duties and claims have been settled. The sum is entirely yours.

'Just collect your legacy, Brit, and try to think kindly of me, which I am sure you often felt like *not* thinking in the past.

'Goodbye, sweet girl. At least Willis named you well

in that.

'Your Aunt Truda.'

Brit put the letter down. She was still staring straight ahead, not wholly absorbing the words she had read, definitely not for one moment believing them, as Cara took the letter up.

CHAPTER TWO

CARA's first impression was incredulity, the same as it been with Brit. The same as with Brit, she read the amount, then read it again.

'That cunning old duck!' she gasped.

'Cara!' scolded Brit.

'She was. Oh, I know she paid her way, but to be sitting on all that. What a slyboots!'

'*Cara!*' exclaimed Brit again.

'Sorry, darling. No, sorry, heiress. For you are, aren't you? It's quite a lump.'

'It's—well, it's a satisfactory sum.'

'It's riches. Why did the old meanie leave me out?'

'You read the letter, Cara. Evidently Aunt Truda was of the opinion that—well——'

'But that's unfair! It wasn't like that at all. It was a different matter with me.' Cara looked at Brit as only Cara could look, and Brit said at once:

'Of course, pet. I agree that Aunt Truda had her own peculiar ideas.'

'With the result that you gain and I——' Tears choked Cara, and she did not finish.

'With the result,' came in Brit warmly, 'that *we* gain, that the family gains. I mean, Cara, Aunt Truda could have left her nest-egg anywhere. Even to an outsider.'

'Yes.' Cara dabbed her eyes and put away the handkerchief. She looked slightly more cheerful. 'Yes, she could.' But presently, caught up in envy again, she repeated: 'Rich!'

'Not really.'

'Well, I could do a lot of things with it.'

'Like?' asked Brit.

'Like—like buying my own small car so I could whiz around looking for openings.'

'An agent can do that for you.'

'An agent can't look like me, and you must admit that looks help sell.'

'Yes,' agreed Brit. With a face like Cara's you had to agree with that. She asked, in the hope of placating Cara: 'What else would you buy?'

'Clothes. Fab clothes. Not the ones you run up ... oh, sorry, Brit, but you understand.'

'I understand.'

'Clothes,' repeated Cara, 'that demand you get noticed.'

'You always look nice, Cara.'

'Nice!' Cara sniffed. She must have decided she was overdoing things, though, for she asked dutifully: 'And you, Brit? What are you planning?'

'First of all goodbye to St. Hilda's.'

'Is that wise? After all, it's——'

'It's good pay, but I won't need that any more.'

'No, *you* won't,' Cara said pointedly.

'Darling, don't be touchy. You're in this, too, of course you are, but St. Hilda's was killing me; I hated it right from the first day Dad ... and Link Wayland—why, yes, it was *him*, remember? ... got the post for me. They thought they were doing great guns, Dad keeping the family tradition alive in a way, Link Wayland believing I could do with extra money, I suppose, but neither considering how I felt.'

'Link,' mused Cara, momentarily diverted. 'I haven't seen him in years.'

'Not since he left the suburb and its local editing for the city rounds. I've heard, though, that he's done extremely well,' Brit said carelessly; she had not liked Link Wayland. She had not cared for the long enigmatical looks he always had given her. It had been all she could do to thank him when he secured her the St. Hilda job.

When the Willis Smiths had settled in Winfield, Link Wayland had called on the family to do a story on the once Australian-known composer of the *Hinterland* ballet for his *Winfield Times*. He had reported graciously on Willis Smith, and Father, Brit remembered, had been very pleased about it, had predicted a fine future for the young journalist.

Whether her father had been perspicacious or merely flattered, he had still been right about Link Wayland. The man had advanced from paper to paper, and, Brit had heard, now controlled a whole suburban series of his own. But she had heard, too, he still took a personal and intimate interest in them all, visited them, advised them, though she had learned this from Aunt Truda, who had mutual friends with Link, and not personally or intimately herself. After Link Wayland had left Winfield she had seen him rarely.

The last time they had spoken was the time her father had to remind her to thank Link Wayland for getting her the posture job at St. Hilda's. Mr. Smith had been gratified that his daughter was not taking on something ordinary, gratified that the money was so good.

Brit had been twenty-one then ... good heavens, had she been 'posturing' for almost five years? ... and Father had said promptingly:

'Brit dear, Mr. Wayland really worked on the St. Hilda trustees for you.'

'I'm sure he did.' Brit had tried to hide a hard frustration in her voice. She must have, from Father, but she had not been so sure of Link Wayland. The man, slightly more mature than twenty-one generally favours, had given her one of those long probing looks.

'Well' . . . a little chidingly from Father . . . '*well,* Brit?'

'Well, thank you, Mr. Wayland. It was wonderful of you, Mr Wayland. I can never repay you, Mr. Wayland,' Brit fairly had burst out.

The dark, almost Indian-bronze six-footer, the man who should have been riding a horse, roughriding it, not writing a leader, and Brit even said so to herself, said it softly, had looked back at Brit with deliberate estimation.

'Just as well you're a dancer, Miss Smith, for you certainly would never make a writer. Far too many effusions. A simple word or two goes as far, and believe me, much more effectively.'

'I'm not a dancer,' Brit had said stiffly.

'She has very nice posture,' Father had come in, not understanding Brit, not understanding the way Link Wayland was talking. 'She'll be a great benefit to the girls.'

'Aged six to twelve,' Brit had said, 'teaching six to twelve how to stand.'

'Perhaps you don't want this job.' It had been said so quietly, so cunningly, that Mr. Smith had not heard.

But Brit had.

'I want the job.' She had known she had gone too far; known, too, he had heard that 'roughriding' of hers. She had said Thank you again, shaken Mr. Wayland's hand, escaped and left Father telling the journalist of other highlights that had happened to him in the hope that they, too, might find publication.

After that they had not conversed again. Brit had

seen Link Wayland sometimes in Winfield—an Indian-red man like he was had to be seen—but she had not acknowledged him.

Aunt Truda had mentioned him often. She had said that Mr. Wayland, whom she met frequently at friend's homes, had asked about Brit.

'A very nice gentleman,' Aunt Truda had said warmly.

Brit had left it at that.

'Yes,' she repeated to Cara now, 'it was Link Wayland who really got me into St. Hilda's.'

'Link,' mused Cara, still diverted.

Brit, watching her, knew what she was thinking. Link Wayland was ... or had been ... the kind of man to appeal to a girl. He had that authoritative, almost dominant way with him that thrills young things. Yet I, too, was young, or youngish, Brit recalled, and I disliked him.

'Strong white teeth against a burnished skin,' remembered Cara. 'Quite a dish.'

She came back to the subject of Brit.

'If you leave St. Hilda's, what?' she asked.

'I don't know. It's all too early yet.'

'Europe?'

'No. A holiday, perhaps, but, Cara, I ... I mean we ... well, there's no actual riches entailed.'

'*One* could do Europe.' Cara's voice was thoughtful.

'And two could go to bed and sleep on it. Yes, Cara, I insist. How otherwise will you perform tomorrow at class?'

'Class!' But Cara did allow herself to be persuaded.

Soon she was breathing evenly in the next bedroom. Cara never allowed herself to carry over any cares. Brit recalled Father telling Cara once: 'Cara means dear, not care. And dear you are, baby, especially' ... with the Willis over-humour ... 'to our pockets. You're a very costly little girl.'

She had always been costly, and Brit supposed that in all fairness one couldn't expect her to change now. She had been reared expensively and now the expensive bud was ready to blossom. It would be a very lovely flower. Brit's eyes as she lay in her bed in her own bedroom grew heavy. She did not expect to sleep, not after all her excitement, but she could feel oblivion approaching. A very lovely blossom, she repeated drowsily, a flower that must have its chance. Giving Cara her chance. Brit slept ...

She awoke to dawn thinly buttering the windowsill with pale yellow. Her first thought was: 'I'm free!'

But she had to go to school to establish her freedom, perhaps in fairness give St. Hilda's a week to find a replacement.

She was brewing the coffee as Cara came into the kitchen.

'Was it a dream?' Cara took the slice of toast that Brit had just buttered for herself.

'No dream. I give my notice today.'

'St. Hilda's, St. Hilda's, you can't ever get away from it, can you?'

'But I *am,*' Brit grinned.

Cara was not in a smiling mood. 'It's all right for you, going in and saying "Count me out,"' she complained.

'I didn't intend those words.'

'You know what I mean.'

'Yes, I do, dear, but Cara, your school is nice.'

'It's a bore,' snapped Cara.

'Until you're ready——'

'Actually, Brit, I think I'm ready now. I believe Madame thinks so, too, she asked me if I would come to superintend a class. Me! A class!'

Brit said nothing.

'Lucky you, sauntering down, sauntering home, filling in time,' Cara went on.

'I have no doubt I'll be expected to work all the week,' Brit assured her.

'With your means you can tell them where to go.'

'But I wouldn't.'

'No, *you* wouldn't, not ever. Brit: Sweet Maiden,' sneered Cara.

'You're Cara meaning dear.'

'I must be, no one has bought me.' Cara yawned and got up. 'Don't spend all your fortune today.'

'I wish you wouldn't keep on saying you and your,' sighed Brit.

'Well, it's not I and mine.'

'It will be.'

Cara actually paused a contemplative moment. 'You *are* sweet,' she admitted reluctantly. She added: 'I don't know how you do it.'

Brit laughed. 'Thanks, pet. For that nice admission. I'll promise I won't spend. I couldn't, anyway, I have to collect first.'

'According to Aunt Truda's letter the cheque is ready.'

'If my resignation is accepted at once I'll go in this afternoon then.'

The resignation was not. Miss Asquith looked at Brit and looked at the same time at a loss. A complete loss. Hadn't she ever heard of legacies?

'This is rather awkward,' she murmured.

'I'm aware of that, Miss Asquith, and I'm willing to help you for a while.'

'You mean with classes?' Miss Asquith said rather vaguely.

What else could there be? Brit thought. She waited for the Head to recover herself.

'Just carry on until I find out, won't you, dear?' the Head appealed.

Find out what? wondered Brit. But she agreed.

She found herself quite enjoying her posture periods that morning, she permitted a lot more windy movements than usual. Helena, who was present again, smiled:

'Mifmif, ith nith today.'

'Thank you, Helena.'

'*You're* nith,' allotted Helena, 'but breaving ithn't, not breaving to one, two, free.'

'Thank you, Helena,' Brit said again.

It was late shopping night, and on the way home Brit bought a celebrating bottle of champagne. When she reached the flat, she saw John's car, and wondered if Cara had broken the news.

When she opened the door it was to Cara and John close together as they studied a page of the atlas. John got to his feet and came across to Brit and held out his hand.

'Congrats and all that,' he grinned.

Somehow it came distastefully to Brit. She wanted him to smile, to look disbelieving, to run his hand through his hair in that surprised boyish way of his. She had always found that a very endearing gesture.

But John just stood very straight ... and somehow aloof.

'A windfall, Brit.'

'Yes.' Odd when you are full of words, words waiting to tumble out, how sometimes only monosyllables will emerge.

'I came to tell you,' began John, and Brit thought: John is finding a *reason* to visit us, visit me; before he just came because he wanted to.

'—to tell you I'll be pushing off quite soon,' John finished. 'If I can place *Southern Cross* overseas I can be assured it will move favourably here.'

'Yes.' Again that was all Brit could find to say.

'And you?' John asked her.

'I?'

'I suppose you'll be changing your address.' He glanced around the small apartment.

'I suppose.' Two words this time, not one.

'Well, I must push off.'

'Dinner?' She was back to one word again.

'I have an appointment.' No—'Will it stretch that far?' accompanied with that John-grin of his.

They looked awkwardly away from each other, Brit knew that she, anyhow, was avoiding John's eyes.

'I'll see you again,' John said.

'Yes, do that,' nodded Brit.

Cara said nothing. She was nail-painting and her attention was on the current colour she was brushing on, a bright fuchsia. But Brit knew she would be missing nothing.

She did miss nothing. As soon as the door closed on John, she said: 'The way people avoid the word goodbye.'

'What do you mean?'

'You won't see John again.'

'Of course I—we'll see each other.'

'I should have added not until after Europe,' Cara amended. 'Perhaps he might turn up later if he becomes rich and successful.'

'He would come poor and unsuccessful.'

'Oh, no, Brit, John's proud. He's one of those old-fashioned men who like their women dependent on them, looking to them for help, not heiressing it all over them.'

'I didn't!' exclaimed Brit indignantly.

'I know, my pet, but it still remains a fact that you have vastly more than John, doesn't it?'

'At present.'

'A very expansive present. It even extends into the dim future. And it could be very dim for John, the same' ... a pathetic break in Cara's voice ... 'as it could be for me.'

'Cara!'

'Oh, I know you say we, you say family, but Brit, it does make a difference, doesn't it? It must, for John saw it, and you must admit that. I see it, too.' Without another word, Cara wheeled round and ran to her room. Brit heard the door shut and then the key turn. Oh, no, she thought, not Cara, too. Not Cara as well as John.

That night Brit did *not* sleep.

But in the morning Cara was herself again, yet not herself really, there was a self-effacement about her young sister, that, had Brit earnestly considered it, had never been displayed before. But all Brit felt was a relief that Cara, anyhow, was friendly.

'This is your toast, Brit,' Cara called as she passed across what she always took first for herself.

'Brit, why did you let me drink all the coffee?'

Then: 'Well, into class, though what they think they can do with poor clumsy little me I don't know.'

Confused, unsure of herself, of what she heard, still obsessed with the subject of John, Brit went to her school, to her posture lessons. But first of all to a word from Miss Asquith.

'I've found out,' the Head said.

'If I'm to last out the week or if I can leave at once?' helped Brit, for Miss Asquith seemed a little awkward, a little uncertain, not at all the self-sufficient woman she always was.

'Last out the week?' Miss Asquith said it, Brit thought, in the same vague way as yesterday she had said: 'You mean the class?' As though somehow it was not the point under discussion. That it was not connected. Brit wondered what else there could be.

'I've found out from Mr. Wayland,' said Miss Asquith.

'Mr. Wayland? But how does he come into it? But of course, he must be a school trustee.' Brit said it more to herself. She knew little about Link Wayland. Probably he was married now and had a daughter booked for St. Hilda's—parents booked daughters well ahead at this exclusive school. He might even have a daughter here now. That was how little she knew about Link Wayland. He could have been married that time he had got her the posture post, she hadn't known ... or cared to find out. But if he had been married he could easily have a child here. She tried to think of any little girl with the surname Wayland.

'Yes.' Miss Asquith's voice was a little faint, but Brit did not hear the faintness. 'A kind of trustee.'

Brit had always thought that trustees were trustees, that no kind-ofs came into it. But evidently she was wrong, and the 'kind-ofs' trustee that Link Wayland was had proved necessary for what Miss Asquith now had to announce.

'You can leave,' said Miss Asquith.

'Thank you—or should I say thank you, Mr. Wayland?'

It was then, Brit thought in retrospect, that Miss Asquith said a rather odd thing. She said, very seriously, very meaningfully: 'Yes. Yes, you should indeed.'

It was odd going out of the big St. Hilda gates in the middle of the morning. As she passed through, Brit met Helena also passing through, but through from the street side.

'I had to go to the dentith,' the child offered, evidently considering Brit required an excuse.

'Did you, dear?'

'Really I'm not late at all.'

'It wouldn't matter if you were,' said Brit. 'I'm leaving.'

'No more lethonth?'

'No.'

'Oh, beaut!'

Brit smiled.

'If only Mif Pidcock would leave, too, and Mif Brown, and Mif——' Helena stopped abruptly. 'But I liked you,' she assured Brit, 'I juth didn't like breaving, and now I'm never going to breave any more.'

'Good-bye, darling,' laughed Brit ... but she wasn't far from tears.

She rang up, made an appointment and went to the solicitors.

Murgatroyd and Mason were very co-operative. They had the cheque ready and repeated to Brit what Aunt Truda had said in her letter, the advice about the wisdom of good annuities.

Brit nodded.

'But,' the partners went on, 'you are a responsible adult and can choose for yourself entirely.'

Again Brit nodded. Ever since last night—and John—she had felt an almost unbearable heaviness somewhere in her. Even with the cheque in her hand, freedom, or so she had thought, in the hollow of her hand, she could not lose that deep depression.

'You're a fortunate young woman,' Mr. Murgatroyd

was saying. 'It's not often that someone of your age comes into such a welcome windfall.'

Welcome? Brit bit her lip. John walking out as he had last night. Cara, definitely on edge, wary, watching, waiting.

'Yes, a very handy sum.' Mr. Mason was adding his piece.

'But still money.' Brit was not aware that she said this aloud, said it rather desperately, until she saw the two men smiling sympathetically on her.

'Has it been so onerous already?' they asked.

Mr. Murgatroyd, the senior partner, began to talk again about investment. 'Some reliable source,' he said, 'that will assure you a safe, steady income, that will support you.'

'You're an attractive young woman,' took up Mr. Mason with a courtly bow, 'but sometimes even attractive young women don't—well——' He looked at Brit in apology.

'Don't marry.' Brit helped him out. She wondered what he would say if she told him that she knew she wouldn't marry, that she had known it last night. It wasn't as if there had been anything definite between herself and John, there had not been, but there had been a warmth, a quiet feeling that one day——

It had gone when John had crossed a room to put out his hand and say: 'Congrats and all that.'

Money. Money meant freedom. But did it have to mean a hollowness inside you as well?

As she went home Brit remembered the celebration champagne she had taken home last night, then forgotten to open. No, she hadn't forgotten, there had simply been nobody with whom to celebrate. You don't rejoice, you can't rejoice, on your own, and after John had left, Cara had run to her room.

As she reached the flat she saw that there was no car, no car, anyway, that belonged to John. But when she reached the hall, the light was on.

'Come in,' called Cara sweetly. 'You're home.'

Chops were grilling.

'Guess what, I told Madame I'd take a class. I announced it this afternoon,' Cara said over dinner.

'But, Cara,' began Brit, 'now that there's no need to——'

'There is need. It's your money. You must use it. Travel, get yourself a nicer apartment, spend. Yes, Brittie, you must.'

'But last night you said——'

'I regret last night.'

'And I,' said Brit in sudden passion, 'regret everything. *Everything!*' Choked up, she rose from the table and ran to her room.

Brit always had had a sense of humour, and even in her emotional shutting of her bedroom door a moment afterwards, even in her burst of tears, she could not help herself from half crying, half giggling: 'Now it's my turn to slam doors, stage a performance—what a perfect sister act we would make!'

But the act hadn't even started, Brit knew happily. The relieving tears stopped at last, she reached her decision. It was her money, Aunt Truda had said so, even if she had accompanied it with advice. It was still hers to do with as she pleased.

And it was not, and Brit felt herself smiling, really smiling, for the first time since John's leaving, going to be prudently invested in any annuity.

It was going to be invested in . . . well, life, one could say. Assuredly, she knew, it was to be invested in love.

Brit did sleep that night.

CHAPTER THREE

In the morning Cara was the same wistful, sweet, effacing figure.

'Brittie, don't do that again,' she begged. 'Not ever, ever again.'

'What, Cara?'

'Don't shut the door on me.'

'You did it with me,' Brit pointed out.

'I,' admitted Cara frankly, 'am irresponsible. I'm spoiled rotten, Brit, thanks to Mother, Father, you. What I am, you've made me.'

'And made a lovely job.' Though she didn't quite understand this Cara, the change was refreshing, and, anyway, Cara *was* a lovely job.

Her sister went off to classes without her usual whine. Brit watched her go, a reed-slender girl with titian hair hanging shining to her slim waist. She had amber eyes to tone with the hair, a faintly tawny touch to her perfect skin. A scintillating golden girl.

I, mused Brit, am surely the brown moth.

Cara even had made an attempt to do the breakfast dishes, but Brit had stopped that. She picked up a saucepan and looked at herself in it now Brown hair, brown eyes, the same skin tone as Cara but with none of the golden glow. Sallow, Brit supposed. Her features were inelegantly blunter, her proportions sturdier, though that might have been because she was not as tall as Cara. However, and with a rather wry satisfaction, since all it seemed to have gained her was a posture class, she stood and moved quite well.

She put the saucepan down. The flat seemed very quiet. It was the first time, Brit realized, she had been in it on a working day. She wondered how it felt to do nothing, that is nothing except housework. Not that she intended to be idle permanently. The legacy was not that big, and besides, she would get bored. If she was married with a family, then it would be a different story. She fell to planning, as she always had from a child, for she had always loved children, her small beloved four. Two boys like ... well, like John. Brit felt her cheeks grow warm. Then a couple of little Helenas, maddening though they might be, for she felt she could not have coped with more Caras.

Yes, little Helenas, not up to pronouncing s's, Helenas she would teach to walk beautifully, but in play, never in lessons.

I'm wasting time, Brit told herself, and she tidied up the apartment. To her amazement Cara had made her bed.

Now into Sydney, but not to Murgatroyd and Masons to tell them she would take their advice, that she would put Aunt Truda's money into an annuity, but to much more interesting assignments. Like travel agencies. Like boutiques.

It was late afternoon before Brit realized it, and, because she seemed to have accumulated so many parcels, she took a taxi home instead of the bus.

Cara was just walking up the apartment drive, and her eyes widened at Brit alighting from a cab. If she resented her sister returning from town in comfort while she fought for a seat, there was no sign in the welcome she gave Brit.

'Darling, how sensible of you!' Her shining gold eyes were looking at the parcels.

'Wait till you see what I've bought,' Brit said

mysteriously.

'Yes.' Now, if Brit had listened, there was not quite so much affability in Cara's voice. However, she sat on the floor beside Brit as Brit opened bag after bag.

'But, Brittie,' Cara said after a long pause, 'this isn't your size.' She was looking at a gold creation, definitely, and everyone would know it at once, a creation for Cara. 'Darling,' she said sympathetically to Brit, 'you must have forgotten—you're a twelve, not——'

'I might forget that,' smiled Brit, 'but I'd never forget what you are.' That was true. Brit had made all Cara's clothes, made them tastefully, though scarcely ever satisfactorily, that is satisfactorily for her sister.

But you would not have suspected that now. Cara's large gold eyes positively glittered.

'You mean ... oh, you can't mean ... but Brit, but Brittie dearest, you always made the cutest things.' As she spoke Cara held up the garment and shivered with pleasure.

It was good to watch her. Brit brought out more parcels, laughed as Cara positively pounced on them with shrill little squeals of rapture. She was every inch a girl, Brit thought.

'But everything is for me, just everything! Darling, you haven't bought yourself one article.'

Only that article called love, Brit knew. She felt happy again. John had gone, but he would come back. He had been dismayed at her changed circumstances and she had let him go dismayed. Next time she would be wiser. As for Cara, she would make no such mistake with her.

'Ear-rings,' she said happily. 'They're not junk, Cara. Perhaps not as precious as they could be, but——'

'Oh, Brit! Oh, *Brit*!'

After that came the pleasure that Brit had kept for

last. Nothing actual this time, but the prospect of actuality. The prospect of a trip abroad—for two.

'You mean——' gasped Cara.

'Both of us. You could take extra lessons in Europe, get a final finishing touch. I would be home in the garret waiting to feed you.' Brit smiled. In her heart she thought: And somewhere there'll be John, striving after his career, needing to be fed—and loved—too. Oh, I'm glad I've decided to follow this path. To receive love you must give it. Annuities!

There were actually tears in Cara's eyes, for once she was beyond words. She put her arms around Brit, something she seldom did, and for a few moments just remained there.

'Why?' she asked at last.

'Why what, Cara?'

'It doesn't matter,' said Cara, and began turning over the brochures.

'It mustn't be all work or you'll be a dull girl,' laughed Brit. 'We must see all the renowned places between your lessons.'—See John in some of those places, Brit dreamed. The Opera House in Vienna, perhaps, John with them in one of the white and golden boxes. The Rhine, and John half-closing his eyes as they sailed past the Lorelei, hearing errant tunes that could be adapted to movement, that *he* would adapt. San Marino curling up a hill. Budapest.

'Oh, yes,' said Cara.

She turned over the travel folders with delight, exclaiming at some of the luxuries that were offered.

'I'm afraid, Cara, that for the two of us it would need to be tourist,' Brit put in.

'Of course.' Cara turned over the page, but she turned it more slowly, almost with estimation.

They had not thought about dinner, but eventually

hunger did nudge them.

'I never bought anything,' said Brit with shock, for she never had done such a thing in her life. 'I tell you what, Cara, we'll eat out.'

'In Winfield?'

'You could have said that once,' Brit reminded her, 'but what about that new restaurant that's opened?'

'The Rembrandt? But, Brit, it's not Winfield, even though it's in Winfield. It's Sydney. It's big city. What I really mean is it's out of town dining, never just a suburban offering.'

'Who wants a suburban offering?' grinned Brit. She felt a little intoxicated, and yet the celebration champagne she had bought yesterday was still tightly corked. She told Cara about the champagne and they giggled together.

'We'll keep it for some future occasion,' Brit said. 'Tonight we'll have the champagne poured for us.'

'I'm wearing the gold. Why not? The Rembrandt is that sort of place.'

'Why not, except I won't match you.'

'Oh, Brit, you should have fixed yourself up as well.'

'Too ashamed to have me tag along?'

'You idiot, you always look nice.' Cara, with the knowledge that tonight she would look beautiful, said it generously, so generously indeed that when Brit put on her long black skirt and the demure white lace blouse she almost persuaded herself she was pretty.

But when Cara came out——

'It has to be a taxi,' Brit barely breathed. Looking at Cara, she was beyond any other words. She crossed to the phone.

But what she forgot, and surprisingly Cara too, for Cara was knowledgeable about such things, was the necessity of booking a table. The Rembrandt, as Cara had said, was not just a suburban offering, it was a cordon bleu establishment. And there were no tables left. The manager said it proudly, if, looking at Cara, a little regretfully. Every night there were press cameras here, rotogravure reporters on the look-out for a known face, or a pretty face, and this girl in shining gold——

Cara was near tears in her disappointment. Brit, knowing her young sister, knew she was still young enough in her lack of self-control to stamp her foot and insist on entry. But for that knowledge, she would not have accepted the offer that came with a soft-footed, smooth-voiced waiter. The waiter whispered in the maître d'hôtel's ear, and the next moment it was a different story. They were being guided across the darkened, candlelit room, placed at undoubtedly the best table in the room, a table closest to the floor show, the very good orchestra, undoubtedly under the personal attention of the head waiter.

But still Brit would have refused, but for Cara, and Cara's temper, though she did not know which would have been worse, an outburst by Cara or——

Or sitting opposite to Link Wayland, as, with much deference, Cara and Brit were being seated now.

Unlike with Brit, it was some time before the realization as with whom they were seated came to Cara. Brit had known it at once, known frozenly, known it with intense distaste.

But Cara, dazzled for a few moments, took longer. Then at last she withdrew her glance from the many admiring glances being directed at her, and looked instead to the man who had availed them the table. A man who could have been Red Indian with his territorian bronzed skin, a man with teeth very white in contrast. A tall, broad man. Cara remembered him rather thrillingly, she had always liked dominant men.

'Why, it's Link! Link Wayland,' she claimed.

'It's the child,' Link Wayland said admiringly, and the admiration as well as what he chose to call her delighted Cara. Of late she had wondered if she had been maturing; beside Brit she seemed quite the adult, not a nineteen-year-older, but then Brit, of course, was positively immature. But Link Wayland's 'child' now pleased her. She pouted prettily.

'Oh, no, I've grown up.'

'And very beautifully,' Link said.

'It's such a coincidence,' Cara prattled. 'We were talking about you.'

His brows, two thick black wings, rose; it gave him, Cara decided, a rather devilish look, something, too, she liked in men.

'It wasn't awful,' she laughed, 'well, only a little. Brit was blaming you for St. Hilda's.'

'Ah, Brit.' For the first time Link Wayland turned to the older sister. 'Brit,' he said again, and his eyes probed Brit's.

'How do you do, Mr. Wayland,' Brit acknowledged.

The waiter was pouring wine. There was no time for a second raising of brows, as Brit knew Link Wayland would raise his brows at her formality.

She waited until the wine had been served, then raised her glass with Cara's and the man's. Cheers were said.

Someone caught Link Wayland's eye across the room, Link smiled and nodded back, and the next moment the young man joined them. It wasn't long before he and Cara were dancing.

'That's what she wanted,' Brit said softly, fondly, but said it, she thought, to herself.

'And what Cara wants——' Link said suavely, and left it at that. He was fixing himself a cigarette. For a sophisticated man in a sophisticated nightclub he did it in an inappropriate manner. He actually rolled the tobacco first in his almost tobacco-brown hand. He had always rolled his own, Brit remembered, remembering, too, how, if reluctantly, it had fascinated her. Her father had had a silver cigarette case which he opened and shut with sharp precision, none of the lazy deliberation of the smoker who first moulded the brown weed and then carefully enclosed it. She recalled the whisper of the paper and heard the same whisper now. She saw Link Wayland put the cigarette in his mouth, light it, the scratch of the ignition making a near-inaudible little sound. Then, against her will, almost as though compelled, she raised her glance to the eyes, Link Wayland's dark, probing, estimating yet inestimable eyes.

'Seen enough?' he asked.

She knew she flushed vividly by the sudden warmth in her cheeks. She tried to gaze back at the man, to return his cool stare with hers, but it was hard. Those dark enigmatical eyes made her want to look away. She held out as long as she could then pretended intrigue in the colour of the wine, it was a dark wine, dark as deep red apples.

In a slightly amused voice he informed her of the house and vintage. His tone implied that he saw through her insinuated interest.

He smoked for a few moments, the blue weave from his cigarette spiralled around him in the candlelit gloom.

'I haven't seen you around Winfield of late,' he said presently.

'I've been around,' she replied sparsely. As he did not comment, she said meaningfully: 'I am ... was ... a teacher at St. Hilda's.' That 'was' came out gladly.

The dark brows raised, but that was all ... for the moment.

'You must be like a little grey mouse and stop in your hole.'

'A brown moth, was my father's description.'

'Yes—Willis Smith. What a work that *Hinterland* was!'

'He died ... but you would know that.'

'Yes, I did a piece on him,' Link told her.

She had read it, and it had made her proud, but she wouldn't tell this man.

'My aunt died too. I believe you knew her.'

'I did indeed.' Now his voice was warm.

There was silence for a while. Cara and the young man who had claimed her swung past, and Link Wayland said: 'She certainly is a gorgeous creature.' He switched his glance quickly from sister to sister. 'Has it been worth it?'

'Has what been worth it?'

'Not what. Has Cara been worth all the sacrifices?'

'I don't know what you're talking about,' said Brit flatly.

'Giving Cara her chance,' he said laconically, and ashed the tip of his cigarette.

She looked at him in dismay—how did he know that family phrase? But of course, Aunt Truda.

'Yes,' she said firmly, 'she has.'

'Yet you still grumble.'

'Grumble?'

'St. Hilda's, which obviously you've never liked.'

'No.'

'Then why in hell didn't you tell me?'

'Tell you? Oh, I forgot, you're a trustee or something. Or you have a daughter there.'

'I have not.'

'Then booked there.'

He said flatly: 'I'm a bachelor, Brit.'

'But St. Hilda's——' she began.

'Is in Winfield. It was in Winfield that I climbed my first rung to success, so I felt I had to show some allegiance. If you ask at the hospital you will learn that I also take an interest there.'

'A kind of debt?' Brit interpreted.

'A glad debt,' he nodded. 'From Winfield I kept on climbing. Indeed I've climbed so high you must listen one day while I tell you all about it.'

'Oh, I know you've acquired a suburban paper monopoly,' Brit nodded. 'I've heard that most of your fantastic prosperity is because of the personal interest you still take in every paper. No doubt that's why you're here tonight.'

'No,' he said blandly. 'I came in the express hope of running into you.'

She smiled perfunctorily at the smooth lie, then smiled brightly at Cara and the young man who were returning to the table.

For a while the conversation was general. Mark Gilmour, Cara's escort, said something about a new project of Link Wayland's, an overseas newspaper consolidation. Across the candlelight Link nodded at Brit and she knew he was indicating that this was the rung he had reached now. She took no notice, but Cara's eyes were wide.

Photographers were moving round the Rembrandt. Tomorrow's social pages would read: 'Seen at the Candle Room' ... 'Dining out last night' ...

With a small, rather lopsided smile Link Wayland nodded to Mark, and the young man took Cara off to be posed by every attendant cameraman.

'She'll love that,' said Brit. 'Thank you.'

'You, I rather gather, would not like it, so there's no need for your own personal thanks.'

'No, I wouldn't. Also, I'm not particularly good at thanks. Remember when you got me my St. Hilda post?'

'I'll never forget it,' he assured her.

'It was good money, though.' Brit had to admit that, and this time he did pick her up on that past tense.

'Was?'

'I've left,' she told him.

'Of course. You inherited.'

'How would you know?'

'I spoke often to your aunt,' Link explained.

'Yes, she told me. She quite admired you.'

'Unlike her niece,' he said dryly.

'Does a highly successful man also have to be highly liked?'

'It helps.' Another few moments of attention to his cigarette, then: 'Are you doing what your aunt advised, putting the money into an annuity?'

'My aunt never actually advised that, she only suggested it.'

'Are you?'

'It's none of your concern.'

'Are you?' he insisted.

'Look here, Mr Wayland——'

'*Are you?*'

'No.'

'Then you're not only immature and naïve, you're a fool.'

'It's my money,' she retorted crossly.

'I'm not so sure about that.'

'Then whose—Oh, I see. You're thinking of Aunt Truda saving it for me.' A pause. 'I think of that, too. Do please believe I'm not that heartless.'

'Heartlessness is the last thing I would accuse you of. Just—just crass stupidity.'

'Aunt wanted my happiness, and having an annuity would never have returned me that.'

'How do you know without giving it a try?'

'I know,' was all Brit could think to say.

Cara was finishing her different poses. Mark was stepping forward to take her arm and return her to the table.

'Have you done anything final yet?' Link Wayland's voice snapped urgently across the candlelight at Brit.

'No, though what it has to do with you——'

'Then don't,' he said, all the old dominant authority she so well remembered emphasizing both words. 'Don't, do you hear? Don't, until you talk with me.'

'Mr. Wayland——'

'Link, for heaven's sake. Surely you've known me that long.'

'That's why it's Mr Wayland,' she said coldly.

'My God, young Brit, you're as irritating as you ever were!' He glanced away from her. 'They're coming. There'll be no more opportunity tonight.'

'Any night.'

'Day will do.'

'Any day.'

'Just hold your horses,' he said finally, for there was no time for any more.

Cara, her golden eyes gleaming, came back on Mark's arm. Brit saw to it that there was no other chance to talk.

Cara babbled excitedly all the way home. Mark was a dear, beautifully polished, but he counted for nothing really, not compared to Link. Goodness, Brit, how Link had succeeded. He must be rich. He must be quite fabulously rich. When you were rich, you could do anything, get everyone to jump to your call. Why, she might have sat all night and not be noticed, whereas at a nod from Link——

'You would have been noticed regardless, Cara,' Brit assured her, but Cara's thrill over her new dresses, over the prospect of going overseas, was not now so acute.

'To be that rich!' she sighed.

They went to bed on that note, Cara to sigh enviously before sleep took her, Brit to toss uneasily for many hours before she slipped into an unrefreshing oblivion—Thank goodness there was no St. Hilda in the morning.

'Just hold your horses.' Brit heard Link Wayland's low voice in the silent bedroom. 'Don't do anything final.'

Then: 'Don't do anything until you talk with me.'

And: 'Don't do anything.'

She heard: 'Don't.'

If she had needed decision, that decided Brit.

She told Cara the next morning to cancel the class she had announced she was taking for Madame, but it appeared the class hadn't started yet. Cara said it vaguely as though she had forgotten all about it. Brit shrugged. It didn't matter. All that mattered was that there was nothing to stop Cara going into Sydney, choosing a route, a date, which manner of travel.

'You'll know better than I do, darling,' Brit told her after Cara had nodded delightedly.

'You could come, too,' Cara invited perfunctorily.

Brit could, but somewhere, unadmitted, unacknowledged, only quietly anticipated ... *hoped for* ... was the thought that John might call in.

Cara returned home that evening piled with literature, with tentative bookings, with departure times.

John did not come.

CHAPTER FOUR

John called at the end of the week. It was the longest week Brit could remember. She supposed this was because she was not working now, that she had time to fill in so that the hours passed more sluggishly. Yet with an exciting journey in view surely this should not have been the case. What, then? But there was no need for self-examination. Brit had to admit miserably that it was because of the manner in which she had parted with John.

When she saw his car pull into the apartment drive that evening she felt a rush of joy. She watched John leap from his old roadster, then come round to the other side to help Cara climb out. He must have picked her sister up on her way home. The pair did not look across to the flat, they were talking animatedly together, and for a few seconds Brit just stood looking down on them. Her two dearest possessions, she thought, though John was not that, not her possession, not yet, perhaps never, though something sweet—if elusive—told her ...

When the couple came in, Brit learned the reason for the animation. John had received an overseas cable asking him to present his work personally to a European house.

'It might mean nothing,' the young composer grinned boyishly, 'it probably won't, but this company is a good one, a prestige one, an international one, and just to be asked is something, and ... well ...' He grinned again.

Brit was running out for the champagne. 'I had it

ready before,' she said a little breathlessly, 'only we didn't get round to it. But this time ...' She handed John the bottle to open.

'No, Brit, *next* time.' He said it softly, only for Brit, as he poured then held up his glass to her glass. That was all he said, but it was enough.

Apart from those few quick words for her, it seemed that John could not stop talking about his own good luck. His fare had been paid, he said, and he would be accommodated over there while he showed what he had to sell. Then after that—He gave a little shrug. It could be all it might amount to, he added cautiously, but ...

'But the La Salle Company,' murmured Cara thoughtfully, 'La Salle is just—well——' She spread her graceful hands, her expressive dancer's hands. She looked very impressed.

In the excitement of John's imminent departure, the thrilling reason for it, it was quite a while before Brit realized that she and Cara had not babbled out their news.

'John—' she laughingly began, 'John—a coincidence you'll never believe——'

'Brit!' Cara's voice cut in as conclusively as a sharp knife. 'No, don't jump, sweetie,' she added apologetically, 'it was just a reminder that the percolator is going mad out there.'

Brit had started no coffee, but she hurried after Cara to the tiny annexe.

'Cara——'

'It's nothing, Brit, except I thought what fun to surprise Johnny instead.'

'You mean—over there?'

'Yes.'

'But how would we know where to find him?'

'The La Salle Company!' demeaned Cara of her sister.

'I suppose there would be no trouble, and yes, it would be pleasant.' Brit saw the three of them meeting up in Europe, John's eyes holding hers as they had held them only a few moments ago, warmly, with promise. With the background of romantic Europe after this dingy little apartment room ...

'You think of everything,' Brit laughed. 'I promise you—not a word.'

To make her sudden absence from the room convincing, she did brew coffee.

John did not stop long, he had lots to do.

'When you two go overseas ... when are you going, incidentally? ... you'll understand the rush,' he told them.

That was an awkward moment, but when John did not press for a firm answer, instead talked excitedly on, the moment passed.

The moment passed, too, of his leaving them. A kiss for Cara, but only a hand-press for Brit. Yet in the tight feel of those fingers ...

Cara was silent after John left, silent, anyway, for Cara.

'Everything all right, darling?' Brit asked. She had had so much to do with Cara, she almost could have stated how many more or how many fewer words her sister spoke from day to day. Now Cara was speaking very few.

'Oh, yes. I've a bit of a headache, that's all. I've had a frightful lot of running around.'

'Tomorrow I'll help you. I'll come, too.' She could, now that John——

'Oh, no, Brit, no need for that.'

But there was no need now for Brit to wait on a

ring, look through a window to the car park. She had seen John.

'No trouble, Cara,' she assured her sister.

'It will be for me if you suddenly feel off colour, Brit. As you will, and take my word for it, for you had your shots the day after I did, and I feel rotten now.'

'You don't have to react that way,' demurred Brit. 'Some people don't.'

'The clinic said it was the only way they could judge that the vaccine had taken.' Cara sounded tired and irritable, and Brit supposed her sister could be right.

There was a lot still to be done in the flat; what things they were taking had to be stowed away, the landlord had to be told they were leaving, tradesmen informed, telephone, post office, papers——

'Well, if you can manage, Cara.'

Cara looked covertly at Brit. 'I've done it all along, so I think it might be better if I finished it now.'

'Thanks, pet. If we had any sense we would have dealt locally and there would have been no need for town.'

'I'll survive,' shrugged Cara. 'Tomorrow I'll do a lot of things. Money among them. We'll need oceans of travellers' cheques.'

'I thought of having the bank transfer a sum to London.'

'Making it necessary for us to go to London every time we run out? That doesn't make sense.'

'I suppose not,' nodded Brit. 'Then what?'

'Travellers' cheques, as I said. As a matter of fact, Brit, that was what I wanted to talk to you about, only John came in with me.'

'Yes?'

'It would be much better, the agent advised, for only one of us to carry the cheques. It's easier negotiation here and handier over there.'

'But what if you wanted something and I wasn't around?'

Cara did not reply at once, and when she did speak her voice was carefully careless, if a voice could be that. It was careless enough, anyway, for Brit not to put any undue importance on Cara's:

'Oh, I'll carry them, sweetie, in my name, seeing I'm doing the rest of the business. I'll get them fixed up tomorrow.'

She told Brit the amount she thought, and Brit agreed that it sounded reasonable.

'The rest of my—our money?' Brit asked.

'Leave that to me too. You were right about having a sum transferred, but not to London, I think. You give me a blank cheque tomorrow and I'll ask the consultant. He's very helpful and will advise us on the best course.'

It was getting late and it had been a long day. Also Cara could be right about the vaccine, Brit conceded, for she did feel a little depleted.

'Thank you. Cara, you're doing well—Did your reaction feel like I suspect I'm beginning to feel now?'

'I told you so,' pounced Cara. 'You go right to bed, and stop there. Only, pet, in case you get like I did, or near-did, give me that blank cheque now. Then you can stay in tomorrow.'

Brit did, then went to bed. Her arm was throbbing and she felt a slight nausea. But her spirits were high, as high, anyway, as spirits could be high when you felt less than fit.

... 'No, Brit, *next* time,' she heard John say again. She saw his eyes, warm with hers.

She felt better in the morning, and got up relieved that she was to be spared a reaction after all. But although she came out to the kitchen no later than usual, Cara had already left. Bless her, smiled Brit fondly, she's really keen over this trip. She had never known Cara away so promptly before.

As she did more packing she smiled over yesterday, and how she had waited for the phone, but today——

The phone rang. Brit picked it up and a voice, a woman's controlled, obviously secretarial voice, asked: 'Miss Smith? Miss Brit Smith?'

'Speaking.'

'One moment, please.' There was the usual office background, then distantly but distinctly a timbre that Brit recognized immediately. Link Wayland's.

Before she realized what she was doing she put the phone down.

It was a foolish thing to have done, she knew that at once. Link Wayland would only be scornfully amused at her childish action, he would have his secretary dial the number again.

He did, or at least Brit presumed the ring was his, but, although she knew she would not be deceiving him, that he was too shrewd for any subterfuges she might make, Brit continued her juvenile behaviour. She let it ring.

Intermittently throughout the morning the peal shrilled through the small apartment. Then all at once it stopped persisting, and Brit heaved a sigh of relief.

She did not know what nudged her to look out of the window at the same time as the big black car swept up to the parking area, but she was thankful she did. A quick glimpse of the driver assured her that Link Wayland had not given up, but then that man never gave up, never had, never would, and she should have remembered it. Oh, how she hated him, Brit thought.

She watched him get out, heard him slam the door

with more force than was necessary, then for a few moments she just looked at him, something she had never done with Link Wayland, always she had glanced quickly away. Once more the thought came to her that a man like he was seemed out of place here; he was essentially a western, not an eastern-stater, a man of the outdoors, something to do with horses, somewhere that he could ride free, untrammelled, and . . . with dislike . . . roughshod. A roughrider.

He was pausing a moment to roll one of his cigarettes. She could not hear the dry whisper of the tobacco up here, but she could see the smoothing movement of the long brown fingers. Then she saw him lick the edges of the paper together. That gave her an odd feeling, something she never had encountered before, not with John, no man, something she could not have given a name to, have tried to define. Disturbed, not knowing why or how, she withdrew from the window. Then, surreptitiously, she drew the curtains.

She was shaking a little, and was annoyed with herself for it, as she checked the door. She had barely driven home the bolt when the knock came—definite, imperative, an open-at-once sharpness.

Brit stood there.

He knocked again—louder. One thing, he could not disturb anyone, get the landlord to give him a key, for the entire apartment population, including the landlord, worked and were absent during the day. She was alone in the block. The only fear was that Cara might arrive home, but, glancing at the clock, at this time that was unlikely.

'Open up, Brit, I know you're there!' he called irritably. It was not just a guess, the certainty of his voice assured Brit of that, he *knew* she stood on the other side, and how did he know? How could he?

'You're a young idiot, it's only for your own good, can't you see that if I wanted to get in ... for myself ... I'd take no notice of locks, I'd kick the door in.'—For myself? What did he mean by that?

A minute went by.

'All right, be a fool and reap the harvest!' He said it in cold anger. She heard him descend the steps, heard the car start.

She was back at the window now, peeping down at him. Just as he turned the corner of the drive, he leaned out and raised an arm up to her. Yet he couldn't possibly see her, she knew that. With reddened cheeks she came back into the room.

'Be a fool and reap the harvest.' She heard his coldly angry voice saying that again.

But most of all she wondered about that '... if I wanted to get in ... for myself ...'

For myself? For Link Wayland's self? But what ... But how ...

She brewed tea, did some more packing, dreaded the phone ringing, wished Cara would get back.

Later, much later than the other times she had gone into Sydney, Cara did. The girl looked a little pale, slightly drawn, so evidently she had had a difficult day, too. Cara threw her things down, glanced across at Brit, then heaved a large sigh.

'Bad day?' asked Brit.

'Disappointing. I mean, after getting all emotionally ready——'

'For what?'

'Overseas. Well, *I* did, anyway. I've just been living from day to day for it, and now——'

'And now?'

'Now we have a few more days to wait. We're put back for a while, Brit, there's been a run of bookings, or a strike, or something. Anyway, we won't be going for another week.'

Another week. Seven days of listening for a phone call ... watching through a window. 'Oh, no!' cried Brit desperately. She saw Cara looking at her curiously, so she proffered: 'I'm emotionally ready, too.'

'Are you? But you seemed ... well, as though it wasn't so important to you.' Cara looked a little disturbed, but only a little, and the look didn't last long.

'No. Only I wanted to get away when we planned, not some future time.'

'It can't be helped,' Cara snapped at her; her nerves must be equally on edge.

'No, it can't. Sorry, darling. I suppose it's just anti-climax.'

'I suppose so.' Cara moved restlessly around the room, picking up things, putting them down again. 'I think I'll go to bed,' she said.

'This early?'

'I was up early.'

'Yes, why so early, Cara?'

'Lots to be done. Oh, by the way, I fixed up your money, believing we'd be in a rush. But that can wait till tomorrow for your checking, can't it?'

'Yes, dear.' Suddenly Brit felt as tired as Cara said she was. She told Cara to go to bed and she would bring in a tray, but when she did the girl was already asleep.

Brit stood looking down at her, at the fan of lashes on her cheeks, rather pale cheeks tonight for Cara, who usually had a pretty high colour. Poor little girl, she was disappointed as well. Only Brit's feeling was not really disappointment, and she knew it, it was the feeling of walls closing in on her, Wayland walls. Link Wayland himself was a wall of a man.

'Don't do anything until you talk to me.'

'You're a young idiot, it's only for your own good.'

'All right, be a fool and reap the harvest.'

Brit took up the tray and went out again. She knew she would not sleep, so she found a book and read, read until the small hours. She was nearly drugged with sleep when at last she permitted herself to put out the light.

She wakened to bright daylight, no mere buttering of an early sun, and to the hands of her bedroom clock showing nine.

Nine! She supposed Cara had looked in a dozen times and decided against waking her.

But Cara had not looked in to make that decision, Cara had decided last night. Brit knew this as she read the letter propped against the toast rack. No toast had been made, Brit noted vaguely, the teapot had not been used. Wherever Cara had gone, she had gone in a hurry, no time for even a quick breakfast.

'Dear Brit, Excuse the hurried scrawl. I lied to you about the delay in our booking, there wasn't any delay, just the same as there wasn't any booking. Except for me—us, I should say. For John and for me. We're a poor pair, no doubt about that, only we must *both* make good, not only one of us, Brit, and the way we see it, three will make it harder to achieve than two. I think that you, even though you're hurt at first, will see it that way too in the end. We're leaving together on an early plane. When John presents his ballet composition, I'm going to interpret it for him. Perhaps both of us will be accepted then.

'I'm sorry about the money—you see, Brit, I'm afraid it's *all* the money, all your money, but think of it as an investment, for I'm sure we'll make the top. Then you won't be merely comfortable, you'll be rich.

'Also, just in case you're concerned conventionally, and you're just the old-fashioned sort who would be, we're getting married as soon as we land at—well, wherever we do land. John has a ton of promise, so I know I'm doing the right thing, and John feels exactly the same about me. We'll make a good pair.

'On the financial side, if it helps any, all those lovely dresses you bought for me can be returned. The ones I haven't worn yet, I mean. Simeon of Gowns by Simeon is very co-operative, or so I've heard. I'd love to take them with me, but John made a stipulation about travelling light.

That's all, Brit. Do please forgive

Your Cara.'

A long minute went by before Brit put the letter down.

CHAPTER FIVE

THE janitor came breezing up the stairs, then he began sweeping along the silent corridor, whistling as he worked, audibly grumbling at something that annoyed him now and then. He did this chore regularly at ten o'clock every day, so Brit knew dully that she had been sitting there for an hour.

Some time later she heard the postman inserting letters in the different boxes. He came around noon ... but it couldn't be that time, she couldn't have remained there staring straight ahead for all that long.

She looked up at the clock and saw it was half past eleven. She went out to their box. Somewhere in her muddled mind she thought there would be a letter from Cara saying it was all a joke. She could almost read the words: 'Ha-ha, caught you this time!'

There was no letter, but there was a circular advertising a round-the-world sea trip, one of the firms they had written to when they had first decided on going overseas.

Brit took it inside, sat down and opened it. It was ridiculous looking at it now, but it was something to do.

'See Florence,' it said. 'See Cologne.' 'See' ... 'See' ... 'See' ... She would be seeing nothing, but Cara would. And John. Cara *with* John.

That was the numbing pain. The other part, the money-crippling part, had not occurred to Brit yet. Only Cara and John.

'We're getting married as soon as we land.'

We're-getting-married.

It wasn't true, it couldn't be true. It just didn't make sense. People didn't marry because, as Cara had put it, they felt they were doing the right thing, because their partner had promise, because the other partner felt the same in return, simply a "promise", they married because they loved each other, because they had looked across a room at each other—and known.

Or had only *one* known, had only *she* known? suffered Brit. Had she imagined that warmth in John's eyes, had she heard something that was not really there when John had said: 'No, Brit, *next* time.'

He had said it as he had held up his champagne, and Brit had taken it to mean—She had taken it to mean wedding champagne, arms linked as two people looked deeply at each other.

'Oh, no,' Brit said, and she got up and walked round the room.

She understood now why Cara had cut her short when she had started to announce their journey to John on the night he had announced his journey. He and Cara would already have discussed their plans, and Cara would have feared that John, always a little transparent, Brit remembered achingly, might have revealed what there was between them. What there was ... yet she, Brit, had never seen it. But she remembered painfully once saying to John that Cara was so lovely it was a wonder he had not fallen in love with her. He had replied carelessly, or carelessly she had thought, that: 'I expect every man is a little in love with the world's Caras.'

He must have been much more than a little to have joined forces with her sister, departed with her. That sort of thing was not done on the spur of the moment. It took time. It took deliberation.

Twelve o'clock chimed, and mechanically Brit made a pot of tea. She supposed she had better have something to eat, if you didn't eat you could die. How long would it take to die? She did not know, she only knew that it had not taken long for a dream to die.

The tea revived her slightly. It still could be a joke, she thought, a sick joke, one of Cara's silly kind of jokes. Before I do ... well, whatever I'm going to have to do, she thought, I'd better check. She crossed to the phone.

The Tressider Tourist House where Cara had been making the bookings, or so Brit had believed, said quite bluntly: 'Miss Smith cancelled all the reservations yesterday.' The clerk sounded annoyed.

'Yesterday?'

'It put us to considerable trouble. On some of the the bookings we couldn't refund the lot, after all she cancelled without notice.'—So at least, sighed Brit, Cara had booked at some time. Her note ... among other things ... had said: '... there wasn't any booking.' Her sister must have meant that there wasn't any ... *not now* ... for Brit.

'I see,' she said over the wire. 'Did—did she explain why?'

'Only that circumstances had cropped up, that instead of the attractive stopovers we'd planned they would go express.'

'She said they?'

'Yes.' The voice sounded surprised now, a little curious. 'Who did you say was speaking?'

'It doesn't matter.' Brit put down the phone.

The paper was still outside the door. Brit brought it inside, put it on the table and turned to Flight Departures. There were three lines announcing morning schedules. She took up the phone and dialled the first company. No, they had no Miss Smith on their list. 'A—Mr. Ferris?'

'No Mr. Ferris.'

'Thank you.'

It was the same with Apollo Air, but Glamis—

'A Miss Smith? Yes. Several indeed. There's a Miss Cara Smith. Would that be——'

'Yes, that would be the right one.'

'The other name again?'

'Ferris.'

'John Ferris?'

'Yes.'

'He is also on our papers.'

'Thank you,' said Brit. She cradled the receiver again. So it wasn't a sick joke. There was to be no: 'Ha-ha, caught you this time!' It was true. *True.*

She put her head in her hands. She longed for releasing tears. She longed and even tried, but none came. She sat there dry-eyed for the rest of the afternoon. She sat till steps started up the stairs and down the halls. The apartmentees were coming home again. It was the end of the day.

Darkness stole into the room, it was time for lights, in a dozen flats people were cooking their evening meals. What time was it where Cara and John were—time changed in different countries, Brit thought vaguely, it could be hours forward, or hours backward. What did it matter, anyway? What did anything matter?

Eventually she brewed more tea, forced herself to eat a slice of bread, then went again to her room.

She steeled herself to look into Cara's room. The bed was rumpled and unmade, drawers open, wardrobe open. The new dresses hung in the wardrobe, as her sister had written. She had said: 'If it helps, all those lovely dresses you bought for me can be returned.' But trust could not be returned. Nor John. Gowns by Simeon! Did her sister think they could help?

Brit still did not receive the money impact, or rather the lack of money. It was not until hours later, still lying wide-eyed in the dark room, that at last the fact did occur. She put it aside. Cara would be selfish, mercenary, but she would never leave her sister without something. Undoubtedly she would have helped herself to a lion's share—something Brit deserved, she thought wryly, presenting the girl with a blank cheque like that, but she would leave her an amount at least to start her off again. Start off where? Brit shivered a little though it was rather warm tonight. Start where? *Where*? She could do nothing, she was completely untrained, that is apart from posture, and who, aside from St. Hilda's, would be interested in posture? *And St. Hilda's was out.* She knew fiercely that she never wanted to go back there. Not because of the lessons, though she had disliked them, and never because of the children, since she had loved them, but because of Link Wayland. Link had got her the post, to Brit he was the job. So she couldn't go there again. Thinking of Link made her think of something else, one of the many things that Link had said that night. He had looked across the table at the Rembrandt and warned her:

'Don't do anything final until you talk with me. Do you hear?'

What had Link known ... or thought?

She actually slept, she did not know how, but she did. She got up at dawn to an empty house ... had Cara and John reached their destination yet? ... and went and made herself breakfast. It was the breakfast that really awakened Brit's sensibilities. There was only an inch of milk, understandable when she had not shopped yesterday, only a heel of bread ... but it was food. She made toast of the heel, made it thoughtfully. I must find out how I stand, she thought at last.

The cheque she had given her sister had been a bank cheque, negotiable by anyone, no name given. Her cheque from the solicitors had been in her name, but she had had it altered so that Cara would work on it. Cara had said she had taken out 'oceans' of travellers' cheques, that she would transfer the rest. Then everything would be quite all right, there would be a substantial 'rest' not transferred, otherwise Cara would not have said as she had the night before: 'I fixed up your money, believing we'd be in a rush. But that can wait till tomorrow for your checking, can't it?' Cara herself had suggested any checking. So the money would be there.

In a way, Brit thought wryly, she deserved to lose it—imagine not putting some away, as Aunt Truda had advised. But they had been departing from Australia, abandoning it for years, as far as they knew perhaps for ever. So what was the use of leaving money here?

She waited till bank opening time, then rang the bank that had issued the bank cheque. No, Miss Smith had taken out no travellers' cheques here, but she had spoken of doing so, and as she had seemed in a hurry they had recommended an express firm. They required notice themselves, so they had sent Miss Smith to—They said the name, and Brit thanked them. She rang at once.

Yes, Miss C. Smith had bought cheques, she had taken out—They told Brit the amount.

It didn't make sense at first. It was beyond belief. Cara couldn't take out that much money, it would leave nothing to transfer. It would leave—well, it would leave nothing at all.

Brit asked the amount again, giving her credentials, saying it was important to know. The clerk repeated the figure, and Brit found she had heard aright. Cara had transacted the entire amount.

Now Brit did not sit still and stare ahead, she checked little things she would never have thought of doing before. Like the rent for tomorrow, when it became due. It was gone. Like the telephone box. It was empty. Her purse held a few coins, and as a last thought Cara must have decided to leave her something bigger, for a dollar was left intact.

And that was all. *All.*

No—another letter was left. A brief one.

'I had to have my taxi fare, but you'll be richly repaid, and meanwhile you can go back to St. Hilda's, you did quite well there. One day you'll be glad you gave me my chance. C.'

Giving Cara her chance. Brit looked at the dollar, looked at the letter. No, never St. Hilda's, she determined, even in her desperation she was adamant about that.

But the next day she was obliged to give St. Hilda's another thought. Her father had certainly seen to it that she could do nothing, that is nothing except what personally had gratified him. Theatrical stuff. Not that a posture class was really that, but at least it was not like dressmaking, which Brit could not have done, anyway. Or typing. Any of these occupations. What, then, could she do? If she had even the rudiments of commerce, of selling, of doing any of the many things girls did these days, Brit would not have been so concerned now. Why, she thought, I couldn't even turn my hand ... it should be foot, she thought a little hysterically ... to teaching dancing, since, because of my obvious lack of talent, I was never taught myself. Physical culture? No, you had to know something about that as well.

She supposed she could clean, but cleaning nowadays was extremely competitive, you had to take along with you all sorts of expensive aids. Child minding, too, demanded a more specialized education than Brit had had. There were factories, but mostly you started as a junior, knew all about your machine by the time you reached her age. Nurse-aide? You had to have a first aid certificate at least. I have nothing, Brit sighed.

The next day she faced up to the fact that she must go and ask St. Hilda's to give her back her job. She did not want to, but she had exhausted everything; she only knew about standing straight, breathing correctly while you did, and who else but St. Hilda's would buy that?

So she went.

It seemed ironical that the first one she saw at the school was Helena. Helena with one sock dangling as ever and a smudge . . . as ever . . . on her small nose.

'Helth belth, Mifmif,' Helena said. She must have remembered she was not to say hell's bells because she added hopefully: 'You're not here any more.'

'I may be,' Brit told her.

'Oh, gwief!'

'Don't you want me?' smiled Brit.

'I like you, Mifmif, but not all that breaving.'

'Perhaps I won't be accepted.'

'Yeth,' said Helena brightly.

Miss Asquith was silent as Brit poured out a story of changed circumstances, changed plans. She listened gravely to Brit's request.

'It is rather difficult, we dropped the posture class, you see—I mean, what was the purpose when——'

'Couldn't I start it again?'

'It was never really in great demand, not like the dancing and eurythmics.'

'Miss Asquith, isn't there anything at all? I—I simply must get something.'

Miss Asquith looked at Brit reproachfully. 'You really have been quite foolish, haven't you? You should never burn your bridges, you should have remembered that.'

'Yes, I have been foolish,' Brit sighed.

'I'm afraid that I personally can't help you,' said Miss Asquith.

'The school?'

'I am the school. But——'

'Yes? Yes, Miss Asquith?'

'Please wait here. I shall make a phone call.'

Brit nodded bleakly. 'Anything will do,' she appealed as the headmistress went out.

The school bell rang. Brit heard the classes being marshalled into lines. She heard the singing class trilling scales, the French class reciting verbs.

Miss Asquith was a long time. She was so long Brit began to think she had forgotten her.

Later she heard a car pull up outside. She heard Miss Asquith's voice ... So the Head was still there. She was talking to whoever had come in the car. Brit listened closely, but she could not catch any words. Then the door was opening. Miss Asquith was returning.

And with her a man who was the last person in the world Brit wished to see. Not now. Not ever.

'Well, then——' Link Wayland drawled.

Miss Asquith went out and Link Wayland found himself a chair.

'So Cara's chance cost more than you bargained for,'

he began.

'I didn't bargain,' Brit said, 'you don't bargain on love.'

A long moment went past, then:

'No,' Link agreed. He looked steadily across at Brit and although his dark eyes probed and estimated as ever, there was a certain gentleness there. The gentleness undid her. To her dismay Brit began to cry.

They were the broken little sobs children weep, and Link Wayland thought that she looked only a child hunched up there in the big chair, the tears streaming unwiped down her cheeks. He took out a handkerchief, unfolded, shook, then leaned over and quietly began mopping up.

The first kindness she had received for over twenty-four hours ... it seemed twenty-four years ... was the final straw for Brit. Instead of just a flow of tears, there was a deluge.

The next moment she was on her feet. He was leading her outside, leading her to his big car parked strategically near the door. He put her in the car, pulled across a blind. It was a very luxurious car, Brit noted abstractedly, with many blinds, many accessories.

'I'll tell Miss Asquith.' He was gone, then back almost in minutes. Without a word he started the engine, and they went out of the St. Hilda gates.

He drove, still without speaking, until they reached a fairly secluded park. He stopped the car near trees, took out his makings, then advised:

'You can cry as much and as loud as you like now, only the birds to hear.'

But Brit listened to his tobacco processes instead, to the whisper of the weed in his palm, to the crackle of the paper, finally to the ignition of the match.

'I'm all dried out,' she admitted.

'Good. Tears are a release, but they don't provide a solution. Feel up to accounting me now?'

'I feel all right, but I see no reason why I should account you. I went to Miss Asquith for help, not to——'

'Not to the man who got you there in the first place?'

'I'd forgotten that,' she said dully. 'I'd forgotten you had a say in the school.'

'No say,' he corrected.

'But——'

'Only a say in you.' He looked at her narrowly through a blue weave of smoke.

'A say in me?' she echoed.

'That's it. You see, Brit, and you may as well know this now since it seems you certainly will later, I carved out that job for you.'

'Carved it out?'

'Inaugurated it, established it, thought it up ... oh, find your own word.'

'I think the word is prevailed. I think you prevailed upon the board to start me.'

'Yes.'

'You must have influenced them.'

'Not at all.'

'Then you must have a persuasive tongue.'

'Rather a persuasive pocket,' he amended, and, as she stared horrified at him: 'Yes, I paid for you.'

'You—you——' she stammered.

'Every pay day I provided that sum you got handed to you in your salary envelope.'

'*You* did!'

'Yes.'

'But why, why?'

'Your father had asked me if I knew of anything suitable for you, meaning, I knew at once, something suitable to him.' Link Wayland smiled slightly. 'He said it had to be something——'

'Something acceptable to the composer of ballet music,' said Brit tightly.

'Yes,' Link said.

'But I still don't understand. Why should you have done it just because Father asked it?'

'Good question,' he awarded.

'Is there an answer to it?'

'Yes, there is. I wanted you under my eye ... well, not too far away from that eye, anyway. You see, even then' ... Link Wayland ashed the tip of his cigarette ... 'I'd decided it would be you.'

'Me?'

'As a journalist I must correct you there, Brit, you should say I.'

'You had decided it would be I?' she complied desperately.

'Yes.'

'For what?'

'For marriage.'

'With whom?'

'Mine is the opposite answer this time, I say me, not I.'

'Are we having a grammar lesson?' she demanded crossly.

'If you like.'

'I don't like. I want a reply. A marriage ... my marriage with whom?'

'With me. I just said so. Your marriage with me.'

He put down the cigarette and waited for Brit's reaction.

CHAPTER SIX

WHEN Brit did not speak, when she just stared dumbfounded at Link Wayland, the journalist drawled: 'Now you're going to say "You're mad!"'

Brit still did not speak, for she *had* been going to say that.

"Mad," Link continued blithely, "and I, according to romance fiction, which incidentally I also have tackled, since, as a determined writer, I've been through the entire gamut, from advertisments to articles to what-have-you—'

'According to romance fiction?' Brit reminded him.

'I answer: Yes. Mad for you.'

'Only,' Brit smiled narrowly, 'you're not.'

'Only I'm not.'

'Then?'

'Then?' he inquired maddeningly, thick brows rising.

'Then why have you done all this?'

'I eventually came to a stage in my career,' Link told Brit leisurely, 'when marriage became strongly advisable.'

'I can't imagine a man like you ever finding it that.'

'It is surprising,' he shrugged, 'but it's still a fact. I needed ... indeed had to have ... a wife. I could have done with one in my provincial days, actually, helping me write up the hospital balls, telling me the correct name of the blue in the matron of honour's gown. I could have done with one when I became a city man.'

'And now what are you becoming?' she asked thinly.

'If I were not modest I would say an international figure. But I am modest' . . . he looked wryly at her and awaited a scornful comment, which Brit did not offer . . . 'so I'll reply that I'm becoming a South American figure.'

'South American?'

'I'm negotiating with a paper complex in Brazil,' he explained.

'How will you manage the Spanish?' Brit asked coolly.

He smiled as coolly back at her. '*Portuguese.*'

'Is it?'

'Yes.'

'Well, it's the same,' she argued.

'Oh, no.'

She felt very ignorant, very immature. She could think of nothing to say.

'I must have my wife beside me when I go to Rio,' he began again. 'It's expected there that a successful man is accompanied by his successful wife.'

'I wouldn't be successful,' sighed Brit.

'Oh, yes, you would.'

'But I've never been.'

'You would,' he persisted, 'you would have succeeded in getting me.'

'Haven't you got it the wrong way round?'

'You mean it should be I got you?—Well, Brit, have I?'

'No.'

There was silence for a few moments. Now Brit could hear the park birds.

'We'll start at the beginning,' Link Wayland said. And he proceeded to do so.

'I always knew what I wanted,' he told Brit, 'right from a kid. My granny reared me, my parents had split up, and Gran used to say: "Link decides what it's to be, then goes after it."'

'Don't tell me you saw me and felt that,' she taunted.

'Believe it or not, I did.'

'But—but why? I'm not——'

'Not your sister Cara? I didn't want your sister Cara. I wanted you. You suited, still suit, me in every way.'

'What way?'

'I like your quiet looks, as a writer I've always gone in for understatement, for the finer, more subtle style, I loathe flamboyance. I like your naïveté—when I require sophistication I can provide it for myself. I like your way of standing, of walking——'

'The posture mistress.'

He ignored that. 'I knew how important it was socially to have a wife who stood like a poppy,' he continued blandly, 'more important than anything else really. To the South American particularly carriage is an estimable thing.'

'I should think there would be many straight-standing señoritas,' Brit interrupted rudely.

'Senhoritas,' he corrected. 'A faint intake of breath after the first syllable.' He paused. 'Ah, but I will have my Senhora beside me.'

'You *are* mad!' she exclaimed.

'No, I just have a neatly pigeonholed mind.'

'And now you're looking into the particular pigeonhole marked Matrimony?'

'Yes.' He decided on another cigarette and went through the usual process. 'Well, what do you say, Brit?'

'No, of course.'

'Of course doesn't come into it. Nor, after we discuss all this, does No. We're going to be married. Were my granny here she would tell you the futility of fighting.'

'Link decides what it's to be, then goes after it,' murmured Brit. She asked curiously: 'Is your name Lincoln?'

'Link. An ironic idea of my mother's that I would join up the marriage again. I didn't. However, the name is a constant reminder that *my* marriage will not be like that one. When we marry, Brit, it's really going to be a link, a link in a long chain of years.'

'I'm not marrying you,' she declared.

'Then,' he asked, 'what are you going to do? We haven't got down to basic facts yet, but we will now. You're broke, aren't you?'

It was useless to lie to this man, so Brit said simply: 'Yes.'

'How much did she get away with?'

'Everything.'

'Everything? Good lord, how in tarnation could she do that?'

Brit told him in a low, unemotional voice; she seemed to have no emotion left.

'You gave her a blank cheque for the lot? Are you quite crazy?'

'I suppose I am,' she sighed.

'Didn't you have any suspicion?'

'Of my sister?'

'Your sister *Cara*.'

'I had love.' Brit had said it before and it had silenced him. But it didn't now.

'You utter idiot,' he told her, 'you stupid little fool.' He was quiet a while, then he ordered her to tell him the exact details of Cara's duplicity.

'You say it all happened several days ago? What have you been doing since then?'

'The first day I think I just sat. After that I did check to see if it was all true.'

'You just sat, you said.' He took her up quickly on that. 'Was the money that much of a blow?' He was looking at her keenly now.

'No,' she had to admit.

'Then?'

'My sister was the blow.'

He nodded thoughtfully, but she could see he was unsatisfied. His sharp journalist mind was seeking something. Presently she knew what he was after.

'Women don't go to pieces over women,' he said extractingly. 'Who else was in this affair?'

'What do you mean?'

'Whom. Whom do I mean.' He was correcting her grammatically again. He asked: 'Did Cara leave the time-honoured letter?'

'Yes.'

He held out his hand.

'It's none of your business!' Brit snapped.

But the hand still remained stretched, and after a moment Brit opened her bag and gave him her sister's note. What does it matter, she thought dully, I can't be any lower than I am now.

She watched him read it, watched his dark face grow even darker, his lips tighten. Then he came to the part that had been Brit's real blow. John.

'John,' Link Wayland said. He read it through again, then, without asking her, he tore it across. 'It's all it's worth,' he said when she went to object. 'Now tell me about John.'

'He's a composer. Something like Father was.' Wayland looked unimpressed. 'He submitted his ballet *Southern Cross* to a European house and they wrote that they wanted to see him.'

'With your sister?'

'No. Cara just went, too.'

'But with John's connivance?'

'You've read the letter,' Brit said sharply.

'Yes, I have. But' ... closely ... '*have you*?'

'What do you mean?'

'Have you read the finality of it?' he asked. 'Accepted the finality? Accepted the oldest writing of all on streets, walls, trunks of trees ... accepted "J loves C"?'

'He doesn't.'

'Oh, I know it's not put that way, I know it's expressed as doing "the right thing", but boiled down it's still come to what *you* wanted with this fellow John, and' ... a shrug ... 'will never get.'

'You're cruel!' she burst out.

'I'm kind, actually, because I'm honest. You've lost him, Brit.'

'I never had him.'

'Then what are you whining about?'

'You'd never understand,' she answered brokenly, 'you only understand words. It doesn't have to be words, you see.'

'That could be,' Link Wayland said surprisingly. 'I'm not what you would call an experienced man.' He looked at her. 'I suppose that amuses you.'

'Why should it?'

'A man of the world! A man who's made a success!'

'I think you've been too busy becoming that success to find time for anything else,' she told him.

'You mean love,' he said bluntly. 'You're right. But I'm a good student. Can it be taught, do you think? Not French Without Tears but Love Without Words?'

'You have a tag for everything,' she said, 'you have an answer.'

'It's *your* answer that I want now,' he told her significantly.

'It's No,' said Brit.

'You don't like me?'

'I don't like you.'

'Apart from that?'

'Apart from what?' she said in disbelief. What else could there be if you didn't actually love someone than liking them? What made this man tick?

'Apart from not liking me could you——'

'No.'

'Then' ... a sigh ... 'we'll begin again.'

'Mr. Wayland, you're wasting your time.'

He ignored her. He started down another road. 'What,' he asked, 'are you going to do?'

'Find a job.'

'At what?'

'I don't know. There must be something, though.'

He shrugged discouragingly at that. 'Is there nothing at all to salvage?' he asked. 'Oh, I know she took the lot, but you must have had a bank balance, you've been well paid throughout the years, Brit.' A short laugh. '*I* know that.'

'Yes.' Brit's nails dug into her palms. 'You know that.'

'Well?'

'There's nothing. Cara's ballet school was expensive. Cara was——'

'Expensive.' He nodded wryly. 'Go on, please.'

'Cara even took her taxi fare.' From Brit's purse, Brit could have added. But she didn't. 'I owe the landlord,' she admitted.

'Are you eating?'

'Only what remains in the house—Mr. Wayland, you're hurting me!' For Link Wayland had leaned across and grabbed her hand, grabbed it roughly.

'I could shake a little fool like you till——' he said hoarsely. 'I could——' He left it at that.

'Well, it's over. I can't alter it. Neither' ... Brit looked at him with finality, or finality she strove for ... 'can you.'

'You mean it's the end of the book. The last period. Full stop. Oh, no, my Brit, you don't get away like that. How, for instance, do you intend to pay me back?'

'Pay you back?' She reddened. She had forgotten all those years of good salary that he had availed her through St. Hilda's. 'But I did work,' she reminded him a little tremulously.

'Yet *I* received nothing from it,' he reminded her in his turn. 'Anyway, passing that over, what about your Aunt Truda?'

'Aunt Truda? But her money had nothing to do with you—she had her own means.'

'Some,' he agreed blandly, 'that I helped her expand. Expand considerably.' He gave a narrow smile.

'You mean you advised her regarding investments?' Brit interpreted.

He did not answer. Intentionally he did not answer, she sensed. She looked up at him, she kept on looking. Oh, no, she was protesting inside her, not that, too!

'You didn't give Aunt Truda all that money?' she begged him.

'No, I did not give Aunt Truda the money, I gave it to you. She knew what I had in mind, so she agreed. She was very fond of you, Brit.'

'The—the money Aunt Truda left me was your money?' Brit said again, said hollowly.

'Not all of it.'

'But most of it?' she persisted.

'Don't let it worry you,' he advised.

She thought that over a minute, then said: 'But it must be worrying you, that fact that I've lost you the money.'

'I haven't lost. Well—not yet.'

'But Cara has it. Or' . . . knowing Cara . . . 'she had it.'

'I still haven't lost.' He looked meaningly at her. 'I've explained myself,' he reminded her, 'I couldn't be more explicit if I burned midnight oil over it. *You* were my investment, Brit.'

'Then the investment has failed,' she told him. 'I'll try to pay back my salary; also, in time, any money you paid Aunt Truda.'

'And then,' he came in quietly, almost indifferently, 'your father's debts?'

'My . . .' She stared at him dumbfounded, yet not this time in disbelief. For she had often wondered how they had lived so comfortably.

'Yes, your father.' He was silent a while. 'I'm sorry this has come out. I never intended it to. It wouldn't have had you only been reasonable.'

'Reasonable!' she echoed.

'Brit, I decided on you all those years ago. I've never regretted the decision and I don't now. When you marry me I'll hand you an unconditional receipt, I'll pull no more strings.'

'I can't marry you!' she insisted desperately.

'Then I must think of something else. Perhaps find Cara.'

'Cara is married to John.' Brit did not realize that she was actually saying this without pain, but she was.

'Good lord,' Link said, 'not for that, you idiot, I told you before that Cara meant nothing as far as I was concerned. No, Brit, I would simply tell Cara the truth.'

'That wouldn't help you.'

'It could impede her,' he said shrewdly, shrewd because he anticipated the sudden dismay in Brit's startled face.

'Oh, no,' she cried, 'that's not fair—after all, she's young, she didn't know, she had no idea——' Her voice trailed off. He just wasn't listening.

'Yes,' he proceeded coldly, 'I would spoil the chance, or at least hinder the chance, that you, your father, your mother, and heaven knows who else have always been at pains to afford her.

'Giving Cara her chance,' he said harshly. 'No, my dear Brit, not ever any more.'

There was a long silence, and during that quiet Brit rallied her forces.

'But, Link' ... she said his name unthinkingly ... 'it could ruin Cara. She's an artist, and temperamental, emotional. If she was on the threshold of something big it could be the finish for her.'

'Keep on,' Link advised, 'the tears are starting.'

'I know she's spoiled, but that's not her fault. Right from a baby she was doted on, so how could she be any different now?'

'Brit, you have to give me something better than that,' he smiled blandly.

'She's my sister.'

'Still something better.'

'I love her.'

'And,' Link sharply included, '*John*?'

'I think so,' Brit said honestly, 'though there never was anything.'

'Nor will be now, yet you can still plead for Cara?'

'Yes, I am pleading for her, I can't have her told. She's my sister, my baby sister. It's nothing to do with Cara.'

'Except that she's put you into this position.'

'I still love her,' Brit insisted.

'Love!' he said in disgust.

'Yet it exists. I know you can't understand that, can't

believe it, but it does.'

'Then,' Link said, 'prove love to me. Prove your love for your sister.' He looked hard at Brit. 'You know what I mean.'

'Marriage?'

'Yes.'

'With you?'

He nodded.

'What sort of return would you be getting?' she asked.

'Leave that to me.'

'You know that I don't care for you.'

He shrugged.

'I could never love you.'

He shrugged again.

'I—I even dislike you.'

'Hate is your next step,' he advised.

'All right, I hate you. So what?'

'So I still say marriage. But note that I don't "offer" it, Brit, I *say* it.'

'And if I don't, then you go to Cara and John, jeopardise whatever they've achieved?'

'That's a little dramatic, surely.'

'But true. John is very honourable ... oh, yes' ... flushing ... 'he is. He would pay you back every penny.'

'How?'

'His music. And that would involve Cara. The marriage could split up. Marriages do when want comes in.'

'Thus it would be advantageous for you,' he suggested slyly. 'I mean John would be back in the fold again.'

'He was never in the fold,' she sighed.

'You know what I mean.'

'Yes, I know, and the answer is no. I would never want it like that with John.'

'Very well then, you know what to do.'

Another silence enfolded them. Distantly a car roared, but mostly the only noise was the sound of the birds.

'What—what sort of marriage?' Brit asked nervously.

'Are there varieties?'

'You should know, you said your parents——'

'Not one like that,' he came in harshly. 'Also,' he went on, 'never a marriage of convenience—as an author I've always had my tongue in my cheek when it came to that. No two people in the world, no man and woman, can live together without *living*.—You're following me, Brit?'

'Yes.'

'We'll live. We'll be man and wife.'

'I think you mean live but not love?'

'Yes, you do follow me. I'll demand a full life, a man-and-wife life. I'll want children. In return you will be cared for, you will be more than ordinarily comfortable, and your damned sister allowed to keep her chance.'

'Live but not love,' Brit repeated.

He did not speak for a while, then he said carelessly, as though it did not matter one way or other to him: 'One of us, or both of us, can always change our mind.'

'You mean live *and* love.'

'You're coming along nicely,' he smiled. 'I might even make a copy girl of you.'

'Can I have time to think, Link?' she begged.

'There isn't anything to think, is there?'

'But can I?'

He considered a moment, then said: 'Yes.'

'But first of all you're going to get something inside you. You're going to leave your apartment and stay at a good hotel, somewhere where the meals will be brought to you, somewhere where you're not depending on yourself.'

'Yes, Link.' She said it docilely, she could not believe she said it like that.

He evidently could not believe it either. He gave her a sharp, suspicious look, found nothing there, then without warning pressed the car's ignition, reversed into the motorway again, and drovc back to town.

He left Brit at the flat with the direction to be ready by the time he returned from his office.

'I can't have an answer by then,' she protested.

'I meant be ready to change your address, Brit. Your packing seen to, all that. However, as regards the other, I'll expect an answer in the morning.'

'You don't give me long.'

'That's Wayland. Riding roughshod was your description once, I seem to think.'

'I'm sorry,' Brit whispered.

'I quite like it,' he assured her. 'I've never wanted to be an indefinite man.'

'Link decides what it's to be, then goes after it.'

'Exactly. You know' ... consideringly ... 'you're a great deal like my gran.'

'She had brown hair? She was a brown moth?'

'She was——' But Brit did not hear the rest. Link Wayland had started thc big car again, he was manoeuvring it away, whatever he called was lost in the turn of the engine.

All Brit did hear was a reminding: 'One hour only.'

She watched him go.

CHAPTER SEVEN

BRIT did little in that hour. She was still gazing blankly at the clothes hanging in the wardrobe, clothes that all had to be folded and packed, and to which she had crossed dutifully at once ... then never touched ... when she heard Link returning. Goodness, had an hour gone already?

She said so aloud, and he shrugged: 'If the rest of it goes so quickly you need have nothing to worry about.' He looked impatiently at the negligible onslaught she had made, and stepping forward he bundled all the dresses up in one swoop.

'Some of them are Cara's,' Brit protested.

'Oh, so she did leave something? You can sort them out at the hotel.'

'What about our cups and saucers, our pots and pans?' she asked.

'Leave them to the next tenant. Are you ready?'

'You *are* a roughrider,' she said, but it was said rather enviously. It must be wonderful to make clear decisions on things, then act on them.

'I'm beginning to believe that.' He went in front of her down the stairs so that she could pick up the garments he would be sure to drop since he carried so many.

The hotel he had chosen was in a quiet part of the city. As soon as he established Brit, he left her.

'I've ordered dinner to be brought up, breakfast in the morning. After that——'

'Decision?' she asked.

'Decision,' he nodded. 'Good-bye, Brit, until tomorrow.' He stood looking at her a moment longer than was necessary. Then he wheeled round and went along the corridor to the lift.

But Brit sat on at the window that she had crossed to, sat staring down at the traffic. Decision. She had to make her decision. Yet what decision could she come to other than the one he had forced on her? She could never let Cara down, not now, not ever; she had got too much into the habit of love.

The unalterable fact that Link Wayland would do exactly what he had warned her he would do was very clear in her mind. He was a roughrider who thought nothing of anybody or anything, only of his own purpose, and he was essentially a man of his word. If she persisted, she had no second thoughts on what would happen. Cara would be contacted, John would be told, the pound of flesh extracted. Two lives ruined.

The habit of love. Brit kept coming back to that phrase. I've got into the habit of love, she knew, a habit that has lasted nineteen years, ever since Father woke me up one morning and said: 'You have a little sister, Brit, a very beautiful little sister. We don't know yet, of course, but her small hands and shells of feet are so slender and graceful one can almost tell now that she's going to be something special. My little brown moth, you, and Mummy, and I will always have to give our beautiful girl her chance.'

Giving Cara her chance. Yes, the habit of love, Brit accepted, it's too hard to break. Cara has been abominable, but how much of it has been her fault? How much ours? We ... I ... made her what she is, and now I ... I alone this time ... reap the harvest. 'Be a fool,' Link had called from the other side of a door that morning, she recalled, 'and reap the harvest.'

Link had seen what she could not see—he had suspected Cara's duplicity. But then he was an onlooker, he was not involved, he had not learned that habit of love. According to Mr. Link Wayland, he never would. Live but not love, he had stated. He had said that that would be their pattern. Then Brit remembered something else that man had said. 'No two people, no man and woman, can live together without *living*—You are following me, Brit?'

Brit gave a little shiver.

But she was woman enough to know that he spoke a basic truth, she knew that the elemental facts of life were the strongest facts in all existence. She knew, too, she really would not want it any other way. Life was beautiful, and life was to be *lived*. Only ... a little sadly ... she had always thought of it more as the end of a lane, a sweet conclusion that you finally reached because coming at last to it was the only natural, only loving thing that you wanted, that you asked for. That you then received.

'Oh, John!' she whispered brokenly.

Dinner came up ... then she realized that once more she had had no effect on the clothes that Link had thrown carelessly on the bed. Her own clothes were intermingled with Cara's. Many more of Cara's than hers. But they could wait till the morning. Tonight was for decision.

Later, lying in bed, the clothes tossed to the floor, staring through the window at a segment of navy blue sky, Brit knew she had come to her decision. Link had not left her any alternative, but even if he had she knew she would not have availed herself to it. Marrying Link Wayland would be advantageous, to say the least, and any advantage she gained would find its way in the end to Cara. That habit of love, she sighed, resigning herself for a night of wakefulness.

The next thing she knew was the sun finding its way by some miracle around soaring city buildings to poke yellow fingers over the bedroom sill. She had slept after all, it was yesterday's tomorrow. Link, she half smiled, who scorned effusion, would have said: 'Use today, not yesterday's tomorrow, don't hedge.' Well, today then, within hours, he would be here to ask her. There was a tap on the door. The maid, Brit thought, with breakfast. She got up, pulled on a robe, and opened up.

It was breakfast, but not brought by any maid. Link Wayland carried it in. Brit saw that the tray had been set for two.

'They were a little surprised, too,' he laughed at Brit's surprised eyes, 'but rather delighted really. That fellow who started "Love makes the world go round" really began something.'

'How does love come into it?' she asked. 'You're only saving the maid a few steps.'

'So unromantic, Brit! Does that portend—No, don't tell me yet. Never tell a man his fate before a cup of brew. Pour, please, Brit. Of course the staff believed love came into it. You're the sugar in my coffee and all that.'

'But you're only interested in life, not love,' she reminded him.

'Two lumps, please,' he directed, 'and love, my child, is for velvet nights, not bustling days.' He glanced meaningly at the traffic now beginning to roar below. Brit, flushing, looked, too. But not for long.

'Link——' she began determinedly.

'Not before bacon and eggs.'

'Don't—don't you want to hear?'

'I want to have something under my belt when I do.'

'But it's all right. It's yes.'

'Wise girl!' He never even looked at her. 'I hate

eating from a tray, it's awkward. Butter my toast, will you, Brit.'

Brit leaned over to do so . . . then she laughed. 'This must be the oddest acceptance in all the world!' She found herself actually giggling.

He put down his knife and fork. 'Laughing suits you,' he grinned. 'Keep it up.'

He looked years younger himself, almost a boy. 'It suits you, too,' said Brit.

'Then we both must laugh and laugh.'

They laughed until the meal was over, and then Brit asked:

'When?'

'The wedding?'

'Yes.'

'Oh, some time . . . I can't tell you exactly yet, you see I wasn't sure myself, so——' He was reaching for his makings.

'But you must have been fairly sure; you knew how I felt about Cara.'

'Yes, your sister was my winning card, wasn't she?' He looked at Brit curiously. 'Tell me, Brit, how does one get like that?'

'Like what?'

'Like all that much loving?'

'The habit of love.' She said it abstractedly, but he picked it up sharply.

'The habit of love,' he repeated. 'But don't habits breed monotony?'

'I think it would depend on the receiver of the love, but I don't know really.' Brit suddenly found she did not want to talk about it. 'You must give me some idea, Link,' she insisted.

'About the wedding date?'

'Yes.'

'Why?'

'Well—I want to be ready.'

'Physically, emotionally or——'

'Don't be ridiculous!' she snapped. 'At least I don't want it to be in a negligée. Like now.'

'I don't mind,' he assured her. He added impudently: 'In fact it could save time.' When she did not comment he told her: 'Not to worry, Brit, unless you're one of those girls who must have a white wedding, all the bridal fal-lals.'

'No, I'm not.'

'Good. I'm not the man to demand it. I covered too many such weddings in my cadet days to require the same myself. So no fuss. Suit you, Brit?'

'It suits me, but all the same——'

'I'll just bowl along and take you to the preacher when I get around to it. Which won't be this morning.'

'I should hope not!' she exclaimed.

He gave her a quick look. 'It would be,' he assured her, 'if I didn't have two board meetings to attend.' He got up, hesitated a moment, then touched Brit's brown head with a light hand.

'Sort out your things. Take a stroll in the park. But don't go getting any new decision ideas, and don't go running away, or——'

'Or?' she dared ask.

'Or I'll drag you back by the hair. Which you'll probably like, anyway. Women, so my romantic publisher told me years ago, like dominant men.'

'I won't get any other ideas, Link—I can't, can I?'

'You mean Cara?'

'Who else?'

'Who else?' He was preoccupied a moment, then shrugged. He went to the door, then abruptly he wheeled back again. He came right up to her, almost only a breath away. 'All the same, Brit, I must extract a promise,' he said.

'What?' she asked, confused.

'Your solemn promise on what we've agreed.'

'I've told you Yes.'

'*Your solemn promise*, Brit,' he repeated.

'You're ridiculous!' she said crossly.

'I want it.' His dark eyes fairly bored into hers. She went as though to withdraw, but he put out a hand and held her. The grasp was iron-tight and it hurt.

'Link——'

'Promise me, solemnly promise me, or by heaven——'

'I promise you.' She stepped back at last, and stood rubbing the painful spot where he had put the pressure. He must be mad! He was mad. She opened her mouth to tell him so, but he had gone.

The maid came and removed the trays. She looked at the bed and Brit knew she wanted to fix it, fix the room. Brit told the girl she was going out.

She strolled downtown, looking into shop windows. One of the boutiques was a bridal one, and that reminded Brit that she was going to be married. Some time, she remembered from Link, when there are no board meetings. That obviously ruled out that flowing white dress she was looking at, and anyway, Link did not want one of those weddings, he had told her so.

What kind, then? Although he might decree it to be quiet and unobtrusive, there probably would be a few people there, editors, newspaper owners, influential important people of the kind Link certainly would know. Womanlike, Brit thought at once: 'What shall I wear?'

As well as getting into the habit of love, Brit had got into the habit of making do for her own wardrobe. She had few clothes, she had had no need at St. Hilda's. When Aunt Truda's legacy had come ... no, not Aunt Truda's, *his, Link's* ... it had been her pleasure to buy for Cara, not herself. I've nothing suitable, Brit thought now.

She began walking again, slowly, thoughtfully. She was thinking: 'I also have no money to buy anything.'

Link, and thank heaven for this, at least had spared her a final humility by not offering her any. Probably he had thought she would have some, even if a very little, somewhere. She had none.

She wandered back to the hotel. The maid had finished the room. She had even hung up the dresses that had been tumbled down. Cara's dresses. Her own. Some of Cara's not even worn yet. As she looked at them Brit recalled Cara's letter. After—the other things, it had said:

'... On the financial side, if it helps any, all those lovely dresses you bought for me can be returned. The ones I haven't worn yet, I mean. Simeon of Gowns by Simeon is very co-operative, or so I've heard ...'

Yes, the firm was co-operative, Brit remembered, for she had bought Cara's dresses herself, and the assistant had assured her that they could be returned. She took them out and looked them over. Perhaps Simeon's would exchange them for something for herself. Cara's dresses were not her type of dresses; also Cara was taller, had different measurements. As she thought this, Brit was encasing the dresses in their individual boutique bags.

She went out of the hotel again.

Simeon was not in the fashionable part of Sydney, in fact the small arcade that Brit entered was definitely shabby. But Simeon, she knew, had no need to go to the people; the people ... smart women, discerning women ... went to him. He was one of the few Sydney prestige couturiers, few since Australia had not climbed the world's fashion ladder as yet, but it was said, and Brit had read it, that Simeon should go far. Go international.

If the arcade was not prepossessing, Simeon's house was a cool tasteful retreat. Its décor was quite perfect, Brit thought, with its cool silvers and serene aquas. It was one of those boutiques where you could browse to your heart's delight, and Brit did now.

Something for a wedding. My wedding. How unbelievable that sounded! She tried the opposite corner to the corner from which she had chosen Cara's dresses. There seemed to be no one in attendance, so until help came Brit put her bags on a lounge, and began rifling through the dresses that were moving slightly in the breeze from the silent fan above the long brass rail.

She liked them all. This Simeon, she thought, had a very gracious line to his designs. This soft amber silk. This dull blue brocade.

'No.' The voice came from so close beside her that Brit actually jumped.

At once the man apologized ... it was a man, not a woman assistant, a man of average height, less than average build, somehow not robust, a man with quietly smiling bramble-brown eyes. John, thought Brit with a small sharp pain, had had eyes that colour.

'I'm sorry you didn't hear me beside you. I wouldn't have wanted to startle you.' He smiled again.

'You said No?' Brit felt at home with this man at once and made her answer to him a question.

'It's not your dress.' He touched the dull blue brocade.

'I know. I'm in the brown category. I should wear the autumn colours.'

'Not necessarily. Blue could be quite wonderful on you, but a more vibrant blue, Miss——?' He looked at her inquiringly.

'Miss Smith. I was here quite recently purchasing clothes for my sister.'

'Yes, I remember Miss Smith on the accounts.' That made them both smile.

Brit laughed: 'A Smith among many other Smiths,' and he laughed with her.

'Now it's your turn?' he inquired.

'Yes and no. I mean, I'm not buying afresh, I'm returning my sister's dresses and hoping I can substitute something for myself.'

'Why not?'

'Aren't you disappointed? I mean, you must prefer new sales.'

'Miss Smith, I'm happy in what I do, but most of my happiness is in other people's happiness. If your sister is not satisfied with the dresses—'

'But she was. She loved them. Could anyone' ... sincerely ... 'help but be delighted with them?' He gave her a pleased look, and Brit finished: 'But she had to go away.'

'These are the returned items, Miss Smith?'

'Yes, Mr——?'

'I am Simeon.' He bowed slightly. 'There is another name, of course, quite as everyday as yours. I'm quite fond of it, I like ordinary things, but I found that my clients prefer the unusual. So' ... he shrugged ... 'Simeon.'

'It is a good name for a salon, and it's a beautiful salon.' Brit paused. 'If your assistant is here perhaps she could tell me if I'm in my right size section.'

'Today she's not here at all. She has the 'flu. Also her assistant and her assistant's assistant have it. No doubt the infection ran the whole gamut.'

'You escaped?'

'So far,' he nodded.

'So you're by yourself?'

'Yes. Would you care to help?' He laughed.

Brit laughed back. 'I wouldn't be much good, I'm afraid, but so long as you don't mind me helping myself now.'

'When I'm here to do it?' he reproached. He gave her a long estimating look. 'I know the size,' he said, 'and the type.'

'You're very astute,' she commented.

'It's my trade.'

He was veering Brit to another corner, his fingers under her elbow were impersonal and yet somehow involved. At the rack he paused and looked at her again.

'These are all the correct sizes, but you haven't said what kind of dress you want.'

A little uncomfortable, Brit said: 'Is that necessary?'

'You wouldn't wear a sun-dress to a dinner party.'

'I'm going—to a wedding,' she told him.

'Morning? Afternoon? Four o'clock? Five?'

'I don't know, I mean—'

He smiled gently at her uncertainty, but he did not press her.

'Friend of the groom? Of the bride? Very close or mere acquaintance?'

Brit said hesitantly, yet knowing she could hedge around no longer: 'I'm the bride.'

He nodded slightly and smiled again. He had a nice smile, Brit thought, a smile that touched his eyes as well as his lips. There was warmth in it.

'Not formal?'

'I ... well, you see ...' Brit bit her lip. 'As a matter

of fact,' she admitted with a rush, 'I don't know myself. Now' ... a little challengingly ... 'laugh.'

'Why should I? I find it quite enchanting. Why should a bride worry about such trivia as formality and the like when there are the important things to be remembered?'

'Like?' Brit half whispered it. There was something intrinsic about this man that made it easy for her to speak at once on a subject she would not have spoken to others in years.

'Like seeing his face ... or her face,' he said eloquently, 'every time you look around. Like lighting a candle in your heart every time you say his ... or her ... name. Oh, yes' ... a self-effacing laugh ... 'I would have liked to have been a poet. But I didn't have that art. So instead ...' He extended his hands.

'Your gowns are poems,' she told him.

'Thank you.' A pause. 'So the dress is for your wedding?'

'Yes.'

'Then it must be something very special.'

'No,' Brit said. She was as surprised by the single word as he was. He half-turned to select a gown, but at once he turned round again. He looked at her.

'I'm sorry, Miss Smith,' he said gently.

'I'm sorry I said it,' Brit returned.

They both shifted the dresses along the rack.

'This should suit you,' he advised at length. It was a pale primrose chiffon he offered, barely primrose, almost only a buttered cream.

'Yes, I like it.'

'Will you try it on?' He nodded to one of the cubicles.

'Yes.'

As Brit pulled the curtain he called: 'Will you let me see it on you?'

'Yes,' Brit said again.

The dress fitted perfectly, nothing needed to be altered. She came out to where he waited. He studied her a long time, then he asked her to walk.

'Yes.' There was a half-sigh with the affirmative. 'Yes, it's you.'

'Thank you for finding it for me,' she smiled.

'Thanking you for making of it what I had in mind.'

'Do I?'

'Oh, yes, yes!' He spoke sincerely.

Brit went back and changed. She tidied her hair, put on a trace of lipstick and came out with the dress to be wrapped.

'You still have more to choose ... or would you prefer a refund?' he asked.

'I would like more dresses, but not today. Can I choose again?'

'Please,' he said.

He put the gown into a box printed Simeon.

'Why,' he said unexpectedly yet somehow not intruding although such a question should intrude, 'is the gown not to be special?'

'It's not a special marriage,' she shrugged.

'A pity.' There was silence a while, and then he asked, still intimately yet never intruding: 'Why does a lovely girl not marry especially?'

'I'm not lovely,' she protested.

'You're beautiful, Miss Smith, you're just what I——' He smiled ruefully and shrugged. 'I'm very rude,' he told her presently. 'It would be your right in your turn to ask me why I'm designing dresses when I could do other things.' He shrugged again. 'Many people do.'

'And what do you say to them?'

Now he laughed. 'The truth, I'm afraid. That I can't do other things.'

'You mean poetry?'

'And active things. Men's things. Unhappily I'm not strong. But I like my work and when I see a dress I've dreamed up come to life on someone like you, then I love it. I loved it just now.'

'Then that's good.'

'Yet not good enough, for it doesn't happen often enough. Why,' he repeated, 'does a girl like you—'

'I could say money,' she suggested.

'But it wouldn't be true,' he suggested back to her.

'Yes, it is . . . in a way.'

'Then find your money elsewhere.'

'Like you—can I say Simeon?'

He nodded.

'Like you, Simeon, I can't find it elsewhere.'

'That I could never believe, not with your grace. What were you, a ballerina?'

'Not even in the corps de ballet. No, I taught posture.'

'I can believe that. You move like a wind through trees—why are you laughing?'

'I taught that to the class.' Brit laughed again ... but she was not far from tears.

'And that's all your gracefulness availed you?'

'Yes.'

'But modelling, surely. A model is extremely well paid.'

'I don't think I'd be right.'

He was looking at her with professional estimation. 'Perhaps not for every house,' he said, 'the trend now is for staccato action, the graceful sweep is out. But you would be ideal for some of the more serious haute couture. You would be ideal for mine.'

She looked at him with interest, and he nodded.

'Gowns need a certain person,' he said. 'For my

gowns you would be the right person.'

'Well,' she said a little wistfully, 'even though I can't do it, it's flattering to know I could have. Thank you, Simeon.'

'Are you sure you can't?' he came in carefully.

'Very sure.' She smiled. 'Are you sure in your turn you did want me?' She tried to make it flippant, but he answered her gravely, sincerely.

'Quite sure. I would pay you a salary of——'

Brit, who had opened her mouth to stop him, stood with her mouth still parted, nothing said. Then: 'That's a lot of money,' she doubted.

'To speak in the jargon they do now,' he said rather boyishly, 'you're a lot of girl. By that I mean you have everything—everything, anyway, I would want.'

'You're not serious,' she protested

'I have never been more serious in my life. I've been looking for someone, Miss Smith. This is not a sudden urge. It has to be the right person, the person you are. I could tell it at once. I offer you that salary now. I even offer you a future partnership. I could do with you. More than that, I want you.' He waited a moment. 'It's early yet, I've taken you by surprise, but if you would think about it—'

'I can't!' Brit said with a half-sob. 'I can't.' She turned blindly and went for the door.

He came after her. 'Your gown,' he told her, and handed her the box. 'Also don't forget the other credits on your returns—And if you can bring yourself to it, do consider what I've said, will you?'

'Why,' asked Brit in sudden desperation, 'have you said it too late?'

'But many married women, indeed most married women, follow a career.'

'Yes.'

'Also you're not yet married.'

'No.'

'Then——'

'Please,' said Brit, and this time she did leave the salon. She even started to run.

She heard his voice as she went along the arcade.

'Consider it,' he called in a low yet reaching tone. 'Consider what I've said.'

Brit emerged from the arcade and the city hum drowned out the voice.

Now the shops could not divert her; she kept on thinking of the salary he had just offered, the possibilities it opened up for her. She kept thinking what she could have done with her life instead of——

'It's not too late.' She did not realize she had said that aloud until she saw someone looking curiously at her.

She went back to the hotel, and with every step her resolve began to build. This is my chance, she thought, Simeon is my chance—why, he even spoke of a future partnership, I could do even better than that very attractive salary he promised. I could save, save very quickly. I could pay back Link Wayland, add the interest he would no doubt expect, I could buy my way out of this—this nightmare, I could——

And that, she knew, was what she was going to do. Marriage was final—well, to her it was final. Link Wayland had let it be known how he felt, too. 'Not,' he had said harshly, 'marriage like that of my parents.'

She did not like the man. More than that she knew she near-hated him. He was all the things she loathed in his sex, dominating, authoritative . . . a roughrider.

No one could make her do anything; he couldn't, the only pull he had on her was money, money to stop him from dealing instead with Cara, and she now had, or could have, money.

She had reached the hotel by now, and she ran up the steps. When she got to her room it was to find the door unlocked and half open. She went questioningly in ... perhaps the maid still had not finished. Link sat on the bed.

'Where in tarnation have you been?' he complained. 'I've waited almost an hour.'

'Was I to be kept a prisoner here?' she snapped.

'I expected you to go out, I said so, but not for this long.'

'Was I wanted, then?'

'Yes.'

'Is it Cara? She's got in touch? She's——'

'No, not your sister, your fiancé.'

'Fiancé?' echoed Brit.

'Yes. Link Wayland, the roughrider. Remember?'

'Why did you want me?' she asked, disappointed.

'For our marriage,' he came back, 'in' ... he looked at his watch ... 'exactly half an hour.'

'It's not true!' she gasped.

'It is.'

'You're joking!'

'It's arranged for less than half an hour. A second has elapsed. Just you, I, the minister, someone pulled off the street for a witness. Also, of course, the background of a church.'

'People aren't married like that—I mean, they don't run in for a few minutes the same as they would run into a shop for a pound of butter or—or for a reel of cotton.'

'We're booked in twenty-five minutes,' he told her firmly.

'No!'

'I'm sorry you want something more formal, Brit, but this has to be it.'

She looked at him wretchedly ... nervously as well, nervous because of what she had to say, yet still she faced up, for it had to be said.

'I don't want anything at all, neither formality nor lack of it. Link—Link, I've changed my mind.'

'The hell you have!' he came back.

'I'm serious, Link.'

'What do you think I was when I made you give me that promise? Brit, I meant every word.'

'You can't make me!'

'I'll make you all right.'

'You won't be out of pocket, either.' She ignored his threat. 'I'll even repay you much more.'

'Who's the Midas you have got hold of since leaving here?' He was lighting one of his cigarettes, eyeing her through the blue weave of smoke.

'You wouldn't know him, so the name doesn't matter. He's a gentleman.' She heard him laugh. 'He will employ me, and—and it's not just employment, it's a chance, too, a very remarkable chance. The money is wonderful. I could start repaying you at once. Then there's the offer of a partnership. There's—'

'What about *our* partnership?' Link Wayland broke in.

'We would never be partners,' Brit cried, 'surely you can see that? It's so much better to face it now, not wait until——'

'There'll be no waiting.' He said it definitely, the voice allowed no argument. 'We're being married *now*, Brit, you gave me your promise and by heaven you're keeping to it.'

'What if I——' But she stopped. She had to. He had stepped forward and put his big dark hand across her mouth.

'I'm marrying you now. If you won't walk out of the

hotel to the church, which incidentally is just around the corner as in the song, I'll carry you. If you won't answer the minister I'll——'

'Yes?'

He did not answer that, but his dark eyes bored into hers. 'You promised me and you're not going back on it,' he said instead.

'What satisfaction will you get out of knowing I came unwillingly?'

'It doesn't matter one iota to me so long as you come. And you are coming.' He put his hand under her arm and began impelling her to the door.

'I could scream,' she warned.

'You'd only scream once.'

'Kick.'

'You could, but I think you're a lady,' he said.

'You could be wrong there.'

'I'll try you out.'

He guided her down the passage, pressed the lift button ... and it was as he said, she thought wearily, with hopeless resignation, she *was* a lady. Either that or she could not go through the embarrassment, the humility, of a scene.

'... Do you, Brit ...' she heard in a daze. The church was small and brown.

She answered: 'I do.'

'... Do you, Link ...'

'I do.'

The disinterested witness wandered off again. The minister shook both their hands, then led them to the door.

They came back to the hotel room. And there Link Wayland took Brit in his arms and held her as she never had been held before. Eyes to eyes, lips to lips.

Breath-close. Almost thought-close. He kissed her, quietly at first, and then longer, more fiercely. Hungrily. He lifted her up, held her aloft a moment, then carried her to the bed.

'John,' he said scornfully. 'The nice gentleman. Ghosts, both of them—wraiths, dreams. I'm a man. Your man.'

She turned away from him, she resisted, withdrew ... and then all at once she was not turning away, not resisting, withdrawing any longer. They *were* ghosts, wraiths, dreams, she knew it in a bemused but strangely positive kind of way. This was a man.

But her man?

Sensibility had returned to her. She sat up. Yet she did not look at him.

'Well?' he challenged her. 'You always said I was a tough customer.'

'I said you never considered people, that you rode roughshod over them.'

'A roughrider,' he agreed. He said it almost with disinterest. 'So what?'

'So I hate you.'

'Why do you keep on saying that? The first thing a journalist learns is never to repeat himself in the writing game. I take back what I said about making you a copy girl.'

'I wish I could take back——' Sobs prevented her from finishing.

'But you can't. We're married, Brit. You're my wife. *My wife.*' He was still lying back as he called it, and though she did not turn to look at him she knew he watched her.

Yes, I'm married, she knew dully; married to this man. I've given Cara her chance ... but what chance has this marriage?

What chance have I?

CHAPTER EIGHT

THEY stayed on at the hotel. Link told Brit he had an apartment but that he would want it redecorated now that he had a wife.

'What is right for a bachelor is not right for a married man,' he said. 'That will be something for you to do.'

'Yes, I want something,' Brit agreed.

He had looked at her quickly, had started to say something, then evidently changed his mind.

They had gone out to visit Miss Asquith, visit St. Hilda's, and the Head had assembled all the school and introduced Mrs. Wayland, once their own Miss Smith.

At the outskirts of Brit's congratulatory previous fellow teachers, and the prefects, a small girl with a gym knicker leg dangling had stood waiting to catch Brit's eye. Catch Link's eye, too, it appeared, for Link greeted Helena by name.

'Helena of Troy,' he hailed.

'I live in Braefield. Pleath Mifmif——'

'Mrs. Wayland now, Helena of Troy,' Link directed grandly. But of course the name of Wayland must be grand.

'Mithmith Wayland, I'm marrying an Indian, too,' announced Helena.

'Are you, darling? When?' asked Brit.

'I haven't met him, but I like Red Indianth.' Helena looked admiringly at Link, no doubt very large to a small girl, looked at his swarthy brown-red skin.

'Will you call your little girl Moonlight on the Water?' asked Helena eagerly. 'That wath in a telly movie. I think ith luverly.'

Brit, hiding her laughter, had said diplomatically: 'We'll see.' She hadn't dared look at Link for some minutes, and then when at last she did she found that he was laughing, too.

But not at the Red Indian part, it appeared he was used to that, but at Brit's face.

'So serious,' he grinned.

'You didn't mind?'

'Lord no. But I thought you did.'

'Being married to a Red Indian?'

'Having a daughter so soon.'

'Oh!' said Brit flatly.

'I myself have no objection, because I would prefer a daughter. I have a special corner for girls. Keep that in mind, Brit.'

She had not answered him. Part of her silence had been wonder, wonder that this big tough man would not demand sons. The other part had been the assured way he spoke, as though a family was not just a possibility but a looked-for conclusion. Yet he did not appear father-material.

Link had said they would not bother doing up the apartment yet, not until they came back.

'From South America?'

'I'll be going there alone, Brit, it seems it will only be a quick visit, so too wearying for you. Later on we'll go and take our time over it. Rio is a dream place and can't be hurried. Then once I get you into Brasilia you'll never want to leave all those gems.'

'Are there?'

'Yes. Glorious gems. That reminds me, I never bought you an engagment ring, did I? What stone do you want?'

'Isn't it rather unusual getting an engagement ring after a wedding ring?'

'Isn't unusual the kind of marriage we have? Ruby or emerald?'

'Surprise me,' she challenged.

'I will.'

Presently he said: 'Will you be all right while I'm gone?'

'Of course.'

'It was rather a foolish question,' he admitted, 'but one, I rather gather, that's expected of abandoning husbands.'

'I wouldn't know,' she shrugged.

'I'll feel better about deserting you if you're left in the hotel—that way I'll know you'll eat.'

'Meals three times a day. Am I to be regimented, too, when it comes to going out?'

'I leave that to you,' he shrugged, 'to your discretion.'

'Discretion?'

'You're a married woman now,' he reminded her.

'I didn't think you would be a conventional man, journalists aren't, are they?'

'They're the same as anyone else, like everyone else it takes all sorts. So' . . . a long look at Brit . . . 'I'll leave it to you.' He waited a moment. 'When I come back,' he resumed, 'if you're a good girl you'll be rewarded.'

'If I'm discreet, you mean.'

He grinned. 'How would I know? Would you tell me? No, you'll be rewarded, anyway, by a honeymoon.'

'A honeymoon?' she echoed.

'We never had one—remember I was, and I still am, too busy. But in two weeks' time——'

'Is that how long you'll be away?'

'Yes. In two weeks' time we'll fly to Hawaii. Would you like that?'

'Hawaii ... oh, yes. But why?'

'Why a honeymoon or why Hawaii?'

'Both, I expect.'

'Because I've never had a honeymoon and I'd rather like to find out what it's all about, and because Hawaii is my idea of perhaps the loveliest place in the world. So in two weeks, Brit.'

He flew out the next day.

At first Brit felt a lightness and a relief. It was wonderful not to look across the room to find his dark eyes watching her, revealing nothing of his own thoughts, simply weighing up and estimating her. It was like old times, even better, really, for all she was expected to do was to sit at the hotel dinner table and be fussed over, no more coming home after a day's work again. And not just fussed, either, but quite lavishly spoiled. Brit decided that the staff must have been previously very well rewarded.

They all liked her, however, or seemed to, and they commiserated with her often for being a temporary widow. They tried to cheer her up, jolly her out of the loneliness they mistakenly attributed to her. Then one morning, to Brit's utter surprise ... and disgust ... she knew they were right.

She was lonely. She missed him. She could not stand Link Wayland but in some ironical way she missed him.

Brit had few friends. Her life prior to this new strange life had been taken up by Cara. Entirely by Cara. There were teachers she had liked at St Hilda's, but now there was a barrier, she knew. She could not go back and claim them. They still worked; she had her leisure. She had sensed that difference the day Link had taken her to visit Miss Asquith, she had known that she no longer belonged. Also ... and a rather lopsided smile ... she had felt their faint envy, not because of her obvious comfort but because of—Link. Yes, because of Link. She had noticed them looking at Link, at the big masculinity of him. Unlike Brit, unmistakably they had seen no roughrider in him, only someone they obviously found most attractive. Brit wondered a little over it, she certainly did not find Link that. Yet she might be the exception. Even small Helena had sighed over the Red Indian.

No, St. Hilda's was out.

It was no use sitting waiting for a letter from Cara, she knew her Cara—probably the two notes she had scribbled when she had left were the longest she had written in her life. In the beginning Brit had worried about it, then Link had very sensibly pointed out that no news was good news, that nothing could have happened to her sister without they found out. Because she had no address she could not fill in time writing herself to Cara. John, as she had expected, had sent no word, so even though she supposed she could have contacted the La Salle Company, she would not do so. Link had sent her a postcard, but that was all; obviously he expected no reply from his wife.

Brit struck up a friendship with Clare, the maid, but Clare had her work to do.

Eventually Brit did what she had known ... but not dared think ... all along she would do, what it was inevitable that she do, though she would never have admitted it. She went to Simeon.

The assistants at Gowns by Simeon were back after their 'flu attack, helpful girls who found exactly what Brit sought, made the transaction of substituting Cara's rejected dresses with dresses for herself a simple one. Brit found herself wishing it was not all so easy, otherwise they would have had to consult Simeon.

Then, almost as though he had seen her enter, though he couldn't have, not behind his panelled office door, the couturier came into the salon.

'Why, Mrs. Wayland!' he greeted.

Brit flushed. He had known her before as Miss Smith, and her marriage to Link Wayland had had no publicity, they had not even announced it in the appropriate section of the papers.

'Simeon,' she acknowledged.

She took the hand he extended, then found it was not just to shake her hand but to guide her into his sanctum.

'While Miss Malling is parcelling your dress you can surely spare me a few minutes,' he appealed. 'By the way, you were suited, Mrs. Wayland?'

'As much as if you'd been choosing yourself—you train your girls to think like yourself.' As she was speaking Brit was looking curiously around her, at the large sketching blocks, at the random figures imposed on the blocks.

'This is where the magic begins?' she asked.

'Or the mistakes are concocted.'

'I don't think you make any mistakes, Simeon.'

'No, I've been fortunate.'

Brit had taken up a rough sketch. The girl in the picture was caught in a gust of wind and the wind was lifting the edge of a swirling skirt. 'You spoke about wanting to be a poet,' she said, 'but you never said you were an artist.'

'I'm not,' he assured her.

'This picture——'

'Is to demonstrate the correct fluid use of silk jersey.' He shrugged. 'No, that's the full extent of my talent, I'm afraid.'

'But with training——'

He shook his head, shook it with finality. 'Art, unlike writing, requires certain physical capability. To be brief, in front of a canvas I would be required to stand. I don't think you've noticed, Mrs. Wayland, or if you have generously let it pass over, but I'm something of a cripple.'

She had not noticed, but she did now, there was a difficulty with his left foot. He moved for her and she saw that he limped slightly.

'It's barely more than a hesitancy,' she assured him.

'Thank you, I like to think that, too. I have no trouble with it, except, as I said, the trouble of accepting my inadequacy when it entails restriction in what I want to do.'

'Polio?' Brit inquired.

'Yes. I was six.'

'I'm sorry.'

'You are, aren't you?' He smiled at her.

'How did you know I was Mrs. Wayland?' she asked then.

'I made it my business. It was easy enough—your husband is a very well-known person.'

'How did you know I was here? There's no glass in the door.'

'I can't answer that as promptly. I simply knew.' He said it diffidently.

—Someone else had known, if not diffidently, recalled Brit. Link had stood on the other side of a locked door and shouted: 'Open up, Brit, I know you're there.' Then he had called: 'If I wanted to get in for myself, I'd take no notice of locks, I'd kick the door in.'

The roughrider. So different, so very different from Simeon.

'Your husband is in South America—Oh, no' ... a

smile . . . 'I didn't "sense" that, I read the item in a paper.'

'Yes, he's gone on business,' Brit told him.

'You must be lonely.'

'No. No, of course not. I mean—Well, I suppose I am, Simeon.' She gave a rueful little moue.

'Nothing to do?'

'No.'

'Then' . . . tentatively . . . 'could you do something for me?'

'For you?'

He glanced down at his sketching blocks. 'I'm working from imagination.'

'And doing very well,' she smiled.

'But how much better if I had a model.'

'Your girls——'

'They're kept busy. Anyway, they're not the type I want for this consignment of material.' He brought out a bolt of the fluid jersey he had mentally used for the wind girl's frock.

'It's beautiful.' Brit touched the supple silk appreciatively.

'It's you,' he said. 'So will you help me?'

'I . . . well . . .'

'Please,' he smiled.

Brit looked around her, looked at the interesting things Gowns by Simeon had to offer. She had been bored these last few days. No one to talk to. Nowhere to go. Nothing, as this man had said, to do. It would be fun, she thought. It would be a welcome diversion. Yet still she hesitated.

Then her eyes finished roving the room and rested on Simeon. He looked steadily back at her, and he waited.

'Yes,' she agreed.

She stayed the rest of the day. Simeon would make quick sketches, then she would leave him to work on them and go out and talk to the girls. She got on well with the girls. Once she actually made a sale, and twice she modelled a gown and they made sales.

At closing time she went into the office again.

'Hilary has been saying how helpful you've been.' Hilary Malling was the senior assistant. 'Brit, we haven't discussed rates.' Earlier in the afternoon they had agreed on her being Brit. After all, if she called him Simeon——

'Oh, no,' Brit protested, 'I don't want to be paid.'

'I can't have you otherwise.'

She could see that he meant it, could see he would be bitterly disappointed to let her go, but that he still would. He would be a proud man, she knew. She would be disappointed, too. The day, after her recent days of boredom, had been sheer delight.

'Then dresses,' she laughed. 'This one, perhaps?'

'The whole salon,' he urged.

'You silly man!'

'You——' But he did not go on.

'Stupid girl?' she suggested flippantly, suddenly feeling a need for flippancy, anything but Simeon's quiet seriousness. 'Oaf? Idiot? My husband calls me these names.' My husband. Brit thought with surprise that this perhaps was the first time she had said that.

'Oh, no,' refused Simeon.

In the finish they agreed upon several dresses to be chosen at the end of the week, or before Link returned and when Brit gave up the temporary post.

'Though,' objected Simeon, 'with remuneration how can it be called a post?'

'I've looked at the price tags on several dresses I have my eye on, and they would take me weeks of salary.

What time tomorrow, Simeon?'

He glanced at her, surprised. 'You come when you wish, of course, but note' ... eagerly ... 'I'm not saying *if* you wish.'

'I'll be here,' she promised.

Brit was. She was there early and she stopped late. For the week she went to Simeon's she was not back at the hotel for one dinner. Lunches, of course, were always taken at the salon.

But at night Simeon took her to a variety of places. She found his taste in quiet restaurants was her taste. He had a dislike for show, for gilt, loud orchestras and long menus. He preferred simple bills of fare with a few, but very carefully prepared, offerings.

'We match,' Brit said one evening.

'I've been thinking the same. We're the right blue with the right pink.'

'The right contrast of textures,' Brit laughed ... and then the laugh was dying away, she was looking at Simeon looking at her with his gentle bramble-coloured eyes. John, too, had bramble eyes.

'Brit——' Simeon began.

'Yes, Simeon?'

'I'm going to Hawaii.'

She stared at that. Until he said it she completely had forgotten about her approaching 'honeymoon.'

'I wish you could be there, too,' he went on. 'I plan to present a new idea I've dreamed up against one of those fabulous Hawaiian backgrounds. For Hawaii is truly fabulous. Have you been to that enchanted island?'

'No, but——'

'I wish you could come now. Be my model. I know just where I would place you, the colours I would use, the style.'

'I can't come, you know that, but' ... a little laugh ... 'I'm coming.'

He looked at her in question, and she said: 'It happens that we're going, Simeon. It's unbelievable, I mean the coincidence is, but Link and I are leaving soon after he returns.'

'You and your husband,' Simeon said slowly.

'Of course.'

There was a moment's silence, then Simeon smiled: 'That will be wonderful. I can see you there. I can meet your husband.'

'Yes, you can meet Link.'

'He might even be enthusiastic about my sketching you.' Simeon's voice was so hopeful that some of the hope splashed over on Brit.

'He might,' she co-operated.

But once away from the candleglow of the intimate restaurant, away from Simeon's eager face across the table, Brit saw things in a different light. Especially when Link's card came.

'Am finishing my South American business here in Santiago. Will leave tomorrow at noon. This should bring me home by Thursday noon. A dutiful wife would meet her husband at the terminal. Anyway, Brit, I'll certainly expect that. The location of the scenic side of this card is the Andes, of course. I'll take you there one day. Till I see you—Link.'

Thursday. Thursday was the day after tomorrow. In two days' time Link would be back.

Brit did not know how she felt about Link's return. Her loneliness in the first few days of his absence had surprised her, but after she had seen Simeon she had not felt lonely any more. She was aware of a confusion now, an unsureness, yet in all the uncertainty one positive thing stood out for Brit. Link must not know that she had been attending the salon. There had been nothing wrong in it, an ordinary man would have been pleased for her diversion, even for her rewards for her service, but Link Wayland was never ordinary. She did not want to deceive Link, deception got you nowhere; at some time or other you were discovered and then it became much worse, but for all that knowledge and her uneasy conscience, Brit still knew the salon visits were something she must keep to herself and Simeon. At least for some time yet.

She determined to confide in Simeon the next day. He would be hurt at her appeal, even shocked, perhaps not agreeable, but she must try to paint the picture truly, make him see it her way.

However, Brit had no such oportunity, for Simeon was not there, he was down with the 'flu.

'It's funny how it sweeps right through,' said Hilary Malling. 'I hope you don't get it.'

'I feel fine now.' Brit was wondering whether she could discover Simeon's address, call at his home and tell him.

'Then I hope you'll help us,' appealed Hilary. 'With Simeon away it makes so much more to do.'

What could Brit say? Anyway, she told herself, it would have been foolish to have gone to Simeon's digs even if she knew where they were.

They were very busy that day, there was no opportunity for doubts and self-questionings. Hilary thanked Brit warmly, was saddened when she knew her temporary service was over.

'You've been manna from heaven,' she told her as Brit left.

There was no postcard from Link. Brit had not expected one, he would have started on his return trip by now. There was still no letter from Cara. No word from John.

Brit sat in the hotel room and wondered about Simeon. She decided at last to ring his home, talk with him, and she picked up the directory to find his home number. Then she smiled to herself. An ordinary name, Simeon had told her at their first meeting, but he had not said what it was. Well, perhaps it was better this way. She put the directory down.

She did not sleep well that night. She looked in the mirror in the morning and she hoped the signs did not show. If they did Link would be certain to notice them.

She took a taxi to Kingsford Smith, then waited outside the Terminal Customs. She had timed her arrival neatly but still knew she could have a long wait; Customs were always unpredictable.

She was surprised when the door opened almost at once and Link came out. Yet should she ever be surprised with that man? Undoubtedly he knew someone who could hurry him through first. Yes, that would be Link.

If his prompt appearance had surprised her it was nothing to her surprise at his greeting. Patently oblivious of an audience, he came over to Brit and lifted her up in his arms. She was embarrassed, but one glance at that dark Indian-red face told her that he was not.

'Why the coyness?' he teased. 'I'm your husband, remember?' He kissed her. Then he held her at arm's length. 'Good,' he said, well satisfied, 'you're a bit washed out. You've been pining for me. I didn't want to come back and find you bounding with health.' He glanced round the Terminal. 'It almost seems a waste of time going back to the hotel seeing we leave again tomorrow.'

CHAPTER NINE

HAWAII was a red hibiscus. Hawaii was brown bodies gleaming in the sunlight as they skimmed in canoes over sapphire water. Hawaii was purple mountains, fold upon fold of purple mountains looking down on freeways, soaring apartments, green palm trees and yellow sand. Hawaii was a touch of silk.

As she had had this last impression, Brit, of course, had thought at once of Simeon, Simeon who might be here, too, and who would think of Hawaii as silk, just as she did.

She and Link had revelled in it for a week now. Ten hours after leaving Sydney they had had their first glimpse together, since Link had seen it all before, of the fabulous Islands, looking down, they had seen Kahului, and then Pearl Harbour on Oahu.

After they had skimmed in they had joined other passengers and entered a quaint bus. There was a procession of buses, all joined together, and they had moved off in a single file. Leis had been placed round their necks, pink carnations today, the pretty hostess had said, tomorrow perhaps white oleander, or wild yellow orchids. When Link and Brit had reached their hotel their room had been massed with flowers and ferns.

They had both been weary enough to rest until evening, and then they had strolled out to see the shops, every conceivable type of shop, parking areas serving them with space for thousands of cars.

After dinner, eaten by a tinkling fountain that filled

'Tomorrow?' she exclaimed.

'Hawaii.' He said it with the usual impatience he adopted if someone did not keep up with his mercurial train of thought.

'But tomorrow ... You'll be too tired.'

'I?' He laughed ... and Brit knew she had been ridiculous. This man would never be tired.

In the taxi he handed her the small parcel.

'Shall I open it now?' she asked.

'You'll wear it now. Can't have you going around without an engagement ring.'

'What is it?'

'Open it up, Brit.'

She did ... wondering what he had chosen. He would select, she decided, something that to him was her. A warm ruby? A cool emerald? A quietly glowing pearl? The velvet box had been unfolded from its tissue now and Brit unsnapped the catch. She looked down at the ring, a ring with a stone she did not know but very beautifully set in tiny diamonds. She admired the setting, but it was the stone that fascinated her. 'What is it?' she begged.

'An Alexandrite. You like it?'

'Oh, yes!'

'I do as well, even though it's a two-timer.'

'What?'

He had put the ring on her finger by this and now he slanted her hand to a darker section of the cab. Instantly the stone that merely had fascinated Brit before deeply enthralled her. It had changed its colour to a lustrous purple ... no, it was a deeply shining green ... no, it was——

'It's wonderful!' she exclaimed.

'It's a wonderful cheat. I chose it because it's you, Brit, you with your different faces for different people.'

A little unevenly she asked: 'Which colour am I, then?'

'To whom? To John?'

'To you?'

Abruptly he pulled her hand back to the brighter light. 'There's no luminosity for me yet,' he answered her.

When they arrived at the hotel, Brit went ahead with the porter who carried Link's bags while Link waited a few moments to speak with the proprietor. As they stepped into the lift she could hear Link talking about Buenos Aires, of his impressions.

But the pair must have spoken of other things after she had ascended, for when Link came into the suite some time later his face was thunderous. She wondered why ... but wondered only briefly.

'Now I know why you look so peaky,' Link stormed. 'Once again you haven't been eating.'

'I have been,' she assured him.

'Don't lie to me, Brit, Mr. Devon tells me you haven't been here for lunch or for dinner for almost a week. Lunch I can allow for. You could have it in a park. In some arcade.'

Brit gave an involuntary start at that, but he did not notice.

'But dinner is the meal of the day,' he went on, 'and you chose not to eat it, even though I left strict instructions that you should. Why, Brit?'

'I didn't feel like it,' she evaded. 'I—I wasn't hungry.'

'Why?'

'I've just told you, Link, I wasn't hungry.'

'No, not that, girl, but why weren't you hungry? Could—could it have been that you didn't feel like food because I wasn't here with you?' He said it a little roughly. If Brit had looked at him she would have

seen another kind of hunger, not a hunger i
his lean dark face.

'Yes,' she agreed. She would have agreed to
to save a scene, for she sensed now that th
Simeon would create a scene.

'Brit.' Link was pulling her to him, his li
pressing down on hers, pressing down as they ne
before, not at the air terminal, not even on
wedding night. 'Brit, my girl, my girl. It's been
nable away from you, it's never going to happen a
Not ever again.' Now the lips were in the crook o
throat. How luminously brown his skin was,
thought, surprised.

She felt him leave her to lock the door. She he
him draw the curtains.

'Not ever again,' Link said.

He came back to her.

in the listening space when the guitar players paused with its own silver music, a dinner at which Brit was introduced to the famous coconut pie, they drove to a point above the city to look down on the old Iolani Palace, the brilliantly lit hotels fringing Waikiki Beach. Link paid off the taxi and they walked back under banyan trees so thick that the navy blue night sky was only etched here and there between the dense leaves. There was a heavy honey smell in the air. Frangipanni, said Link, or jasmine.

He had his arm linked in hers, and Brit let it stay there. She could barely see her way ahead, and, anyway, it was that hand-holding kind of night.

'A lovers' night,' Link told her.

Later in the hotel room, the doors flung wide open to the small patio to frame a moon, stars and a corner of rustling palm, Brit could almost have believed that. She fell asleep in Link's arms.

They went sailing in Kailua Bay. They drove round the island to Waimea where the big waves break, some thirty feet high, and here they watched the surfboard riders.

That night they did not return to their hotel, but stayed in an old Hawaiian inn that had enchanted Brit. It was cool and green and quiet, deep in milky frangipanni and crimson poinciana, had a ceiling of woven bark and a grass matting floor. Fountains played in enormous shells.

Link bought Brit a muu-muu and insisted she wore it. Also a hibiscus on the correct side of her head.

'Because you're married now.'

If she had forgotten she would have remembered again on that velvet evening. Just outside their room a bird sang in a bamboo, and suddenly Brit knew she was trapped deep, trapped in something else as well as all this beauty; she felt herself enfolded, she felt a moment grow into timelessness. She knew a strange, sweet, inexplicable joy. And when she wakened she was still in strong yet tender arms.

'Good morning. Have a happy day,' Link smiled. He added: 'That's the authentic Hawaiian greeting.'

She nodded, suddenly blissfully happy, though not understanding it. 'Good morning,' she said. 'Have a happy day.'

When Link said later that he had business to do, that for the next few days she must amuse herself, she looked at him in reproach before she realized it.

'Do you have to?' she asked.

'I always have to. How otherwise can I buy you coconut pies, you little nong?'

Nong was not one of the words she had told Simeon about. Simeon! He seemed a long time ago now.

'All the same I appreciate your concern,' Link grinned. 'It makes you sound like a wife. Wives, I'm told, always complain when they don't receive full attention.' He took out his wallet and handed her a roll of notes. 'Go shopping,' he smiled.

They returned to Waikiki Beach Hotel, and Brit enjoyed herself poking into small antique shops, eating at different national restaurants, buying souvenirs and swimming in the deliciously warm water. She learned to string flowers into leis. She was shown how to float with snorkel and goggles, the only way to experience a new exotic water world. She ventured into native markets, native eating houses.

While Link negotiated for more coconut pie wherewithal for his missus, or so he said, Brit looked beyond the reef to Molokai (the Friendly Isle) and Lanai (the Isle of Pineapples).

Link was home of an evening and once when he was

late Brit surprised herself with her unease. What had happened to him? The cars here moved at a terrific speed—had something happened to Link?

When he came in she actually started to run across to him, then stopped herself. He gave her a long probing look, then said: 'No note of excuse, I'm afraid, but a reason. I met a Sydneysider. I'll tell you over dinner. Put on a muu-muu and wear your hibiscus to prove you belong to me—we're going to Lobster House.'

Lobster House had the background of lovely Mariner Bay. There were flares on the wharf and they lit up yachts, launches, cruisers and fishing boats, all rocking gently now at anchor.

The restaurant was in the form of an old boat, decks, both upper and lower, simulated cargo in casks and crates, many riggings and ropes. The table Link selected had its own porthole and was lit by a red lantern. The menu was seafood, crab, lobster, many varieties of fish. The ever-present pineapple was served with each dish.

Brit smiled over her doggy bag she was handed for uneaten food. 'Doggy bags,' Link explained, were just that, though he wondered if doggies ever received them.

'More like it they're used for that hunger that attacks you in the middle of the night,' he shrugged.

'I'm always asleep in the middle of the night.'

'Yes, little one, I know that,' he smiled, and she wondered if he did know, if he had watched her while she slept.

He ordered coffee and two Daiquiris to have with it, because the seafood left a salty taste in the mouth.

'Rum,' he interpreted to Brit of the Daiquiris, 'with fresh Hawaiian lime.' She tasted hers and proclaimed it delicious.

After he had rolled a cigarette, he said: 'I met this Sydneysider. Funny that, Brit, however international you are you still instinctively turn to your own.'

'Was he your own? It was a male, I'm presuming?'

'Yes. Male.'

'Then was he? I mean, so many people you meet are never your own.'

'You'll like this cove. Come to think of it' ... looking across at Brit ... 'he's your type.'

'What's that?'

'Quiet. I could almost say gentle. But a real man for all that. But never' ... seriously, no smile at all ... 'a roughrider.'

'You don't forget that, do you?' she said.

'Tell me when *you* do.'

'Is this man you encountered in your line of business?'

'No. We met over a coffee break I was grabbing. He was grabbing one, too. Like us, he's over here for a few weeks.'

'But, unlike you, only on vacation?' she said meaningly.

'The nagging wife again!' But Link grinned as he said it. 'No,' he went on, 'as a matter of fact, he, too, is sandwiching in some business. But he has more spare time than I have, and seeing he's by himself, I thought it would be good if he spent that time with you.'

Brit looked irritated. 'You might think that, but I mightn't. I'd sooner be alone.'

'I'd sooner you have someone with you. This island is idyllic, but even idyllic paradises can have a flaw.'

'I'm perfectly safe,' she insisted.

'So far.' Link drank some more of his lime rum. 'Don't be pigheaded, Brit, a woman is better anywhere with a man.'

'Including a maternity ward?' she flung.

'If you like,' he agreed calmly. 'Just let me know before and I'll arrange it.'

'You're impossible!'

He hunched his shoulders carelessly, then went on, 'The two of you could visit some of the other islands—Kauai, Molokai, Lanai, Maui. I'm proposing this because I have to flip over to Los Angeles. I know I said I never would, but something has cropped up. Now don't put on your wifely look.'

'I won't, I'll keep in mind you have to buy my coconut pies.'

'You'll remember more than that, Brit,' he said, 'and that's a promise, not a threat.' He smiled at her flushing cheeks.

'I can go with a serene mind,' he said presently, 'if you agree to be friendly with this fellow.'

'The fellow may not want to be friendly with me,' she pointed out.

A wind had sprung up and the gentle sway of the craft at the end of the wharf had augmented to a busy rock. The lighted flares moved up and down. A lighthouse somewhere sent a beam on a passing ship. Years ago missionaries sailed here, thought Brit; how had they felt when they had come from their cold north to the warmth of the islands? Like: 'Good morning. Have a happy day,' said with both arms outstretched as did the Hawaiians?

Link now was draining his Daiquiri. He said: 'I believe he will, though. I'm sure Sim will.'

Sim. Sim? Brit sat very still a moment.

'Simon, I expect.' She listened to her own voice, a cool, rather aloof voice.

'No, as a matter of fact. Something much less usual, though still an old name. His name's Simeon.'

'Oh.' Brit said no more.

'He's in the rag trade, though rags are the last thing you would call his creations, I'd bet on that without even seeing them.'

'Why?'

'He's elegant. I really mean he's never rags.'

'I wouldn't think he'd be your type,' she commented.

'I wouldn't think so, either, but we clicked at once.'

'And you mentioned me?'

'You came in all the time. Talk about husband-obsessed wives, I'm one wife-obsessed husband!' he laughed.

'*I*'m not laughing,' Brit pointed out. 'Can't you see you're embarrassing me?'

'How? By talking about you? I like talking about you.'

'By making arrangements for me.' Brit added: 'With this person.'

'You'll like this person.'

'Because you like him?'

'That seems as good a reason as any to me.'

'Then not to me. I might take an instant dislike to him.' Brit gulped when she said that. How, she thought, *how* can I go on like this?

'Well,' Link said with sudden indifference, 'you're seeing him whether you like it or not, you're going out with him whether you like it or not.'

'Then what if I do like it?' she flung suddenly. 'What if I like it—a lot?'

'Then that at least will be something, won't it? So far, Brit, you've been anything but a red hibiscus, more a cool rose.'

'With thorns?'

'With thorns,' he concurred. As she sat fuming, he went on: 'I fly out in the morning, I'll be in L.A. till the end of the week. If it interests you at all I reckon this takeover I'm intending will assure you of crates of coconut pies.'

'Meanwhile I entertain Mr. Simeon.' She said that deliberately. It needn't be Simeon, though the coincidence seemed too strong a one.

'Simeon White.'—White was Simeon's name then, that is if it was him.

'I don't think I'll do it,' she said.

'You'll damn well do it, Brit, you'll damn well do what you're told.'

'Told by you?'

'Yes.'

'And if I don't?'

Link caught the waiter's eye and signalled for the bill. They started to the door—then the waiter came running after them with Brit's doggy bag. She left it to Link to take it and went on to the threshold of the pretend old boat, finding no magic now in the rigging, the portholes, the gangplanks.

She looked back and saw that Link and the Hawaiian were talking together ... and smiling. The Hawaiian gave her a quick glance, smiled again and said something to Link, then Link answered. He was laughing to himself as he joined Brit.

'I told him I would probably consume the contents of the doggy bag myself tonight as we'd had a quarrel.'

'You what?'

'But he had an answer to that ... fortunately in Hawaiian.'

'You understand Hawaiian?' she asked.

'I've been here a number of times,' Link reminded her.

'What did he say?' Brit demanded. 'I mean the Hawaiian part?'

'Literally, you want?'

She looked at him and waited.

'Then,' interpreted Link, 'it was: "Ah, friend, but all quarrels are sweet in the dark of the night."'

She started walking quickly, but he hurried and caught up to her. 'So,' he finished, 'we won't need our doggy bag.' A liquid-eyed ragamuffin was sidling along the wharf. Link gave a whistle and sent the bag through the air. The small boy caught it deftly and raced off.

'Now,' and Link turned to Brit, 'we'll see if our Hawaiian was right.' He nodded to a taxi and gave the name of the hotel. Inside the cab he finished: 'We'll see if all quarrels are sweet in the dark of the night.'

It was morning, and Link had left. Brit must have been asleep when he had gone, for she had heard nothing. She would not have known now but for the empty place in the bed and the quick note:

'Good morning. Have a happy day.' Link had added: 'Also have a good breakfast.'

That at least made her smile, for breakfasts here were unbelievably large. They started, in Brit's case, with guava juice, went on to American hot cakes and maple syrup, sliced turkey, eggs, fresh crumbly bread and a long pot of coffee. Have a good breakfast, he had said!

She sat on at the patio table. She did not know quite what to do. Link had let her know last night that he had meant what he had said about Simeon White. She was to meet him ... or at least he was to meet her. She was to go out with him.

Once again she had dared: 'If I don't?' at Link, and Link had silenced her with his lips.

But he had found a moment to warn: 'Then I'll thrash you, my darling, just as I'll thrash that Benjamin.'

'Who's Benjamin?'

'He was our waiter at the Lobster House, the one who advised me that all quarrels are sweet in the night. Yet shall I judge him too promptly? Too soon? Stop quarrelling with me, Brit.' He had drawn her inevitably to him.

Now she drank more breakfast coffee. Perhaps if she went out as soon as she was finished she would miss Simeon; no one moved around early in this Hawaii. It seemed inevitable that she met him eventually, but the longer she put it off . . .

She drained the coffee, then tried to get up. But she found herself sitting on. Sitting on. She tried again, still sat. I must go, she willed herself, I must. Link will be mad with me, but it's much better to avoid something, or at least to postpone something, until——

Then she saw it was too late. She saw Simeon moving among a thicket of palms only some fifty yards away, stopping, as Simeon would, to unfold a leaf, to look into its green hollow.

There could still be time if she moved at once, if she went down to the beach. Simeon would inquire at the desk, but if she wasn't in the hotel then—then she just couldn't be found.

But he had seen her. He was hurrying, almost running, across the perfect green lawn.

Brit had left the table to go to him. They met under a bank of brilliant creeper; he had come down some twisting steps beneath fern and bamboo and had crossed to the sundrenched wall.

'Brit!'

'Simeon!'

'It's a dream!' he exclaimed.

'It's true,' she smiled.

'It's a dream that I'm here . . . and so are you.'

CHAPTER TEN

BRIT and Simeon went over to the terrace table. The waiter had cleared away the remains of Brit's breakfast, and now the tall Hawaiian came across and smiled at Simeon.

'Good morning. Have a happy day. Coffee, perhaps?'

'Coffee.' Simeon smiled back at the man.

When he had gone the two under the gaily striped umbrella simply looked at each other.

'It's a dream,' Simeon said again.

'It's true,' Brit repeated herself.

Seats under other umbrellas were filling up around them, so Simeon guided their conversation into less personal channels. He looked around him, looked at the shimmering quality of the morning. A very good morning; such good mornings had to be happy days. Simeon said so, adding:

'I want to capture it, I want to put sunshine, blue water and green palms into the swing of a dress. Does that sound ridiculous to you?'

'No, Simeon,' Brit assured him.

'If I had been Gauguin in Tahiti I would have sought out a special kind of pink. I'm not Gauguin, I'm Simeon White taking a working vacation in Hawaii and wanting to express myself in—well, in a rag.' He looked ruefully and humbly at Brit.

'No, never a rag,' Brit refused, and she remembered that Link had refused that, too.

Simeon said gratefully: 'You believe in me, don't you?'

'Oh, yes.'

The coffee came and they sipped it silently for a while.

Then: 'Why, Simeon?' Brit asked. She knew he would understand what she meant.

'Why didn't I say to your husband: "I know your wife, Mr. Wayland, she modelled for me last week, we dined together, we——" '

'Yes, Simeon. Why?'

'I don't know,' he replied.

A long moment went past. Then:

'I simply don't know, Brit,' Simeon said again. 'I just liked him ... he's quite terrific, but then you'll be aware of that, of course.'

'No, I don't believe so.'

'Then wake up, Brit,' Simeon advised.

'This is still not telling me why you started an intrigue, Simeon.'

'Did I? I suppose I did in a way. But I just couldn't say it somehow. I couldn't, Brit.'

'Yet *why*?' Brit still persisted. 'There was nothing to tell. I mean, it could sound like something, but really it was nothing, nothing at all.'

'*I* know that,' nodded Simeon, '*you* know that, but *Link*——'

'Oh, so you two are on first-name terms,' she observed.

'Yes,' he nodded, 'we took to each other at once.'

'And you think Link would not know it?' she probed, returning to their discussion.

He shrugged. 'That could be. It could happen like that. And—well, I just liked him too much, Brit.'

'Yes, you said so before.'

'I like him so much,' continued Simeon after a short pause, 'I wouldn't want him hurt.'

'He couldn't be, he's not the type, he's—he's a roughrider.'

'Oh, no, my dear,' Simeon protested.

'You don't know him, I do. Anyway, Simeon, what was there to tell?'

'Nothing, as you said.'

'Then——'

'Nothing apparent. Only——'

'Yes?'

'Only that I love you, Brit.' Simeon had lowered his voice, but he still spoke clearly and she heard every syllable. 'Only,' he continued still in the low but distinct voice, 'if I told him anything, anything at all, I know that love would have to show. It must show, Brit.'

'But, Simeon——'

'I'm sorry. That's how it is.'

She looked incredulously at him. 'Simeon, I can't believe you.'

'I love you, Brit,' Simeon said again.

They finished the coffee, they walked side by side down to the beach. They were amused . . . or they would have been amused if they had not been preoccupied . . . with the grass matting to walk on right to the water's edge. So different from the beaches of Australia, Brit said absently.

'Yes,' nodded Simeon just as absently, 'sand between the toes is an expected thing there.'

They sat on a rock and watched the bathers. There were no large waves at Waikiki, the sea swirled softly up and withdrew again almost in a long blue sigh.

'You don't really love me,' Brit endeavoured rather weakly. 'I was just the first one to do justice to your new fabric.'

He leaned across and pressed her hand as it cupped and then trickled out sand. 'We'll leave it at that, then.

Thank you for the reason, Brit. Now what do we do this week?'

'What do we do?'

'Link has asked me among other things to take you inter-island. He has been there himself and is particularly anxious that you go as well.'

'Haven't you been before?'

'No. I've only ever visited this island, this Oahu. The tourists' island, you could say. Apart from Honolulu I really know very little, yet that little was sufficient to lure me back. I barely even know Waikiki.'

'Then I'll show you that,' she offered eagerly.

'I hoped you would. Then when we finish we can see Maui and Hawaii, Hawaii that gave the islands its name. We'll be seeing them for the first time at the same time. I like that. Do you?'

'Yes,' said Brit, cupping more sand. She wondered if all this was really happening.

First of all it was Brit's turn to show Simeon what she had discovered here. Although he had been a visitor before she had, he had not, as he had confessed, seen much.

'Then what did you do with yourself?' Brit teased. 'Daydream?'

'As well as sketch. And I hope now to sketch you. With' ... quickly ... 'a view to a new design. I told your husband so and he approved.'

'Did he?' said Brit, a little surprised. 'What did you say?'

'I didn't actually say, I showed. I handed him my sketchbook and at once he offered your services.'

'Yes, Link is very good at doing things with other people.'

'You sound bitter. Don't be bitter, Brit, it's not you.'

'I know,' she rebelled, 'I'm Greek for sweet, I'm a sweet maiden.'

'You are indeed.' His smile dissolved her rancour.

They decided to start their explorations that afternoon. They began by doing all the little shops, Simeon being particularly interested in the silk screening the islanders presented so enchantingly. It seemed sacrilege, Brit sighed once, to come out after fingering material with the feel of petals as well as the design of petals to eat at an authentic Japanese restaurant where they cooked their own steak and onions at the table and dipped it in the sauce of their choice, but that was Hawaii and particularly Honolulu.

They inspected the coral, the fish reserved in a bay enclosed by the reef, then decided at last it was time to see the other side of the Hawaiian Islands. It was not the Hawaiian face that most tourists see, and Brit felt excited as she boarded the inter-island plane with Simeon. Link had recommended Maui and Hawaii as real Pacific islands, undisturbed much by the visitor and the busy trend of city life.

It was not far across, and because they had not come to see a town, any kind of town, they made at once for the mountains, passing pineapple fields on the way tended by Japanese planters wearing large coolie hats. There were also cowboys on horses, but their driver said that here they were called paniolis.

Simeon had his heart set on seeing the crater Haleakala, a dormant volcano.

'Its name means House of the Sun,' he told Brit dreamily. 'Legend has it that the sun was once imprisoned there.'

The volcano was some ten thousand feet and around

the six thousand mark the trees became sparse and the bushes stunted; it seemed unbelievable after all the previous lushness. But it did not last long, for the simple reason that two thousand feet higher they could see nothing, they were part of a cloud. The driver pushed on, Brit could not have said how he did it, and then they were above the cloud and could look round again.

It was magnificent. It was clear up here, though half-way down clouds still hung to the mountainside. The driver showed them the distant island of Hawaii, the largest of the group so that it had given its name to them. He told them that unlike Haleakala, or House of the Sun, there the volcanoes did not sleep.

Brit stood a little behind Simeon as they looked down on Haleakala. What did Simeon see in the House of the Sun? she wondered. She only saw internal fire, a rising and a subsiding. But Simeon seemed fascinated. Instinctively he put out his hands.

'I thought I'd lost you,' Brit laughed on their way down again.

'I felt at peace. Crazy, isn't it? I felt—I felt strong, Brit.' He gave a quick, rather embarrassed laugh. 'According to our brochure we now see three-hundred-year-old drawings. We sit under a hundred-year-old banyan tree.'

Brit peered ahead. 'I would like a cup of tea at that five-hundred-year-old edifice ... or is it only four hundred and fifty?'

'It's the disused gaol, so you won't have tea there, only ghosts.'

But, as Brit presently declared, they were nice ghosts.

'No baddies, I think, Simeon, just roistering sailors or peace-disturbing natives.'

'Now who's crazy?' he laughed.

They had found a tea place on a small bitten-in bay, the water lapped rhythmically as Brit took up the pot and poured. The smiling girl had brought freshly sliced lime instead of milk. The tea was deliciously refreshing.

It was halfway to sunset. The mountains were putting on their purple but the sky was pink, red and bright orange. It was timeless, somehow. Although they sat alone there, Brit had the sensation that they were part of a large company of Hawaiians long gone, Hawaiians who, too, had listened to the silver lap of the water, looked at the purple, pink, red and orange.

They walked together back to the small inn that had been provided, companionably quiet, needing no words. Their hands brushed.

The next day they left Maui for the island of Hawaii, the still-volcanic island. As they approached it they could see the volcanoes. Mauna Kea and Mauna Loa, Brit read from the inter-island plane tourist brochure.

It had been arranged ... by Link, who had done it all before ... that they take the old road along the Honokao coast. There were a few other tourists in their group, and although they were all now on a friendly basis, Brit and Simeon were pleased when they were seated in a small car to themselves.

They rimmed tiny coves with dancing blue water, palm tree gullies and pineapple plantations. Guavas were there for the taking, and several times the driver paused and smiled as Brit tumbled eagerly out to eat the small, red, luscious fruit. She always chose guava juice at breakfast at Waikiki, and now she enjoyed the cherry-like globes that provided the luscious nectar.

Bamboos encroached on them now, waterfalls splayed above them. The island of Hawaii proved totally different to Brit, it had a strangely arresting beauty, not at all like its pretty sister isles. For instance Mauna Kea, which rose over thirteen thousand feet out of lush jungle, showed a powder puff of snow. Snow in the tropics, she marvelled.

The party were to stop overnight in yet another Hawaiian inn. This pleased Brit, for although she revelled in the American-type luxury of the Waikiki hotel, these woven bark refuges, with their cool, their quiet, always a fountain playing in a huge clam, delighted her.

This inn did not even serve its meals at conventional tables, but always spread what was offering on long benches under trees.

What offered at the evening meal astounded the party. Pig that had been marinaded in shoyu and ginger awaited them, freshwater shrimps, mussels and fish. Mostly the fish was raw, but delicately and exotically presented. There was liver, poi, huge baskets of papaya, bananas, melons and berries, and rush flagons of a very fruity wine.

It was a heady wine, and when the guitars began to sing it did not take much persuasion for Brit to join the other ladies in their group in a lesson in the hula. As Brit learned all about the gentle swinging of the hips, the movement of the hands and fingers, the ripple of the arms, she smiled at Simeon watching her, swaying as the other onlookers did to the intoxicating rhythm.

While the guitars rested, or rather by the sense of rising excitement while they got ready for a star turn, Simeon led her to a tiny cascade at the side of the inn. It was a paper moon and tinsel kind of night, almost too unreal to be real. Brit said this as she leaned against a pandanus and caught her breath again. The hula was very exhausting.

Simeon seemed a little abstracted. When he spoke it was seriously, not with a smile as Brit had, not in tinsel strain to match the tinsel night.

'It's all so timeless,' he said, 'I feel I'm in the past, the present and the future all at once. If anything happened to me it could have happened yesterday, today or tomorrow.'

'Oh, Simeon, don't talk like that!' she begged.

'I'm not unhappy. Don't think it, Brit. This last week has been the happiest week in my life. You've done it.' He touched . . . barely touched . . . her hand.

Presently he said: 'I have no one, you know, Brit, no brothers, sisters, no relations at all.'

'Sometimes,' Brit tried to banter, and thinking to herself as she spoke that she spoke a near-truth, as regarded Cara, anyway, 'one is better off.'

'Why I said that, about my being alone, was to explain to you what I've done.'

'What's that, Simeon?'

'An impertinence in its way, I suppose, but—'

'Come,' called a honeyed Hawaiian voice, 'come!' A guitar twanged a summons as well.

In pairs, the group returned to the circle. Lines of lovely dusky girls were waiting for the music. When it came, Brit had to smile to herself at her hula attempt compared to their art.

Then she was not smiling. She was watching with thrall as a quite huge, quite elderly Hawaiian woman came into the centre of the dancers, and then began the swaying movements. Never had Brit seen such beauty, such grace, such tender feeling. Simeon had spoken of timelessness, and this, she thought, was the essence of time itself. She clasped Simeon's hand as she watched the story of Hawaii, the culture of Hawaii, the soul of Hawaii, unfold.

When it had finished, no one seemed to want to talk. Even the guitars whispered into silence. When Brit said 'Goodnight, Simeon,' he nodded his understanding and left as well.

It was only a moment before sleep that Brit recalled Simeon's: 'Why I said that, about my being alone, was to explain to you what I've done.'

What had Simeon done? she thought drowsily. A great pandanus leaf disengaged itself from its parent tree and fell on the roof of the grass hut. Brit did not hear. She was asleep.

The volcano Kilauea was throwing molten lava into the air. It only erupted yearly, at the most twice a year, and then briefly. This time it was a little more restless, their guide had said, and had overflowed the crater so that at night a glittering red snake ran into the sea. No, he smiled to nervous tourists, it was safe.

When the explosion occurred, many of the tourists gravely doubted this. It happened late in the afternoon on the day before their return to Honolulu. Some of them were out in small boats, some of them were beach-combing. Brit and Simeon were sitting under a tree.

At the sound all eyes turned at once to Kilauea. A fountain of fire was rising skyward; it subsided, then it rose again; there were a few rockets of crimson spray.

The guide went from group to group assuring each that it was nothing, the goddess was simply a little annoyed, simply showing off, but that was all.

And it would have been all—save for the minor earthquake the eruption aggravated. Or did the earth-quake aggravate the eruption? Even scientists later could not agree which came first.

One moment Brit was saying to Simeon of the Crater flare: 'It's scarey, but it's beautiful in a way,' and the next moment she was looking horrified at the scene before her. It was all aslant. The little bay was crooked. The banks around the bay bent. There was a rumbling beneath them in the ground. Brit saw some vines collapse, spilling orange petals over grass that all at once had gaping cracks in it. She saw the path to the inn wreathe up, then down like a mythical dragon.

She did not see the tree under which they sat uproot, and all she felt when it happened was a soft flurry of leaves over her face.

But Simeon did not know about the leaves, he only knew the bruising tree trunk bursting down on him. When Brit parted the branches, moved away the twigs, he seemed all right, just a tiny wound in the side of his head. It was an unimportant-looking wound, only an inch or so of congealing blood.

'Simeon!' she cried.

He did not answer.

'Simeon ... *Simeon*!' she screamed.

He opened his lids, and Brit, horrified, could see that his gaze was blurring, his lips stiffening, his eyes beginning to glaze. 'Oh, no!' she cried.

He was trying to say something, and she leaned over to hear him. There were only two words she could decipher. They were '... for you.'

Then Simeon died.

CHAPTER ELEVEN

BRIT waited on the island of Hawaii until Link flew over. The rest of the party had hurried away, even though the area had been declared quite safe. There had only been one victim from the phenomenon ... an earthquake at the same time as an eruption had been termed a phenomenon ... and that was a sad misfortune, the authorities regretted. Had the pair not sat under that particular tree——

One victim—Simeon. Simeon White of Australia. No dependants. No one at all. Brit had answered all this to the officials.

'We have had word from your husband, Mrs. Wayland,' they said gently. 'You are to remain here until he crosses over, then he will take you back himself. Please don't worry. Nothing more will happen. You are quite safe.'

Yes, she was safe. She was also alive. But Simeon ...

'Why?' she asked herself. 'Why?' It was the first thing she asked Link.

'I don't know, darling.' In her numbness Brit did not hear that darling. 'I'm as upset as you are. Even though I wasn't here, and not part of the tragedy, I still feel I'm in it as well. Also' . . . a painful pause . . . 'I feel responsible that he came here at all.'

'Why did he?' she asked dully. 'I mean, why did you tell him?'

Link hunched his shoulders. 'I wanted you to see the islands and it seemed a good opportunity for you to see them with him. My God, when I think that I might have been sending you to your death as well . . .'

Common sense prompted Brit to tell Link not to think that way. Simeon had been keen to come, he would probably have come, anyway.

'I suppose so.' Link was still distressed. Presently he asked: 'How did you find him as a man?'

'Oh—he was nice.'

'I told you so. I knew you two would click.'

'Perhaps if we hadn't——' Her voice broke.

Now it was Link's turn to tell Brit to be sensible. After he had repeated several times that it might have happened wherever Simeon was, whoever he had accompanied, he asked: 'They said . . . the report said . . . you two were sitting under a tree?'

'We'd seen everything. It was the last day; some of the group were boating; some were combing the beach. We were just sitting and talking.'

'Yes, he was an easy guy to talk to. Did you find that, too?'

Brit nodded.

'What happened then?'

'The crater was erupting, it does so once or twice a year. Then suddenly there was this explosion, though the scientists say now the 'quake moved first.'

'It's hard to establish,' nodded Link. 'The 'quake was actually subterranean, some miles away, and only this island received any effect. What else, Brit?'

'Everything aslant,' she described, 'everything bent or the wrong way round. The path to the inn looked like the Loch Ness monster.'

'Yes?'

'Then—then the tree was uprooted, I expect. I never saw it, I only felt leaves on my face.'

'Poor Simeon got the trunk on his chest and head.'

'Link, don't . . . please don't!' she begged.

Link was silent a moment. 'Had you got to know him very well?' he asked.

Brit paused, then said: 'No.'

'A pity. He would have been a good friend. Did he speak before he died?'

Again Brit paused. Then she said: 'No.'

She could not have said why she spoke these lies. Unless, she thought, it was the tightness in her, the soreness in her heart. She wanted no probing finger on that sore heart. Not yet.

'We'll go home,' Link said.

'You mean fly back to Honolulu?'

'Home. Sydney. You can occupy yourself fixing up our flat. I'm sorry, Brit, that it turned out like this. I'm not making much of a success of your honeymoon, am I? Away half the time. Having this happen.'

'You didn't make it happen.'

'No,' he said bleakly.

She wanted to comfort him, to say something to take that strained look away from his face. But she was too saddened herself, and ... and she had to admit it ... she simply did not know how to reach Link. I don't understand him, she realized. I don't even know how to approach him. He is my husband, but I don't know.

They flew out the next day. At Brit's suggestion they went straight to the flat. She felt her hotel days were finished. Besides, the place had too many ghosts of Simeon. For over a week she had come busily and happily down the hotel steps to walk to the arcade to Simeon's. For over a week she had returned from Simeon's. She wanted to get away from the place.

'It's rough,' warned Link of the apartment. 'To suit,' he added obliquely, 'a roughrider.'

'I'll tell you when I see it,' she said.

When she saw it, Brit was surprised.

It was decorated in the usual down-to-earth tans and browns that men went in for, but there were some surprising touches. A French walnut bureau, for instance. A Georgian dropside table. A soft pink marble wash stand.

Also—a photograph.

Brit stood before it and stared in disbelief. It had started out one of Cara and herself taken years ago. It had been taken, Brit estimated, just around the time of her acceptance by St. Hilda's. Cara had been a schoolgirl, and that was probably why she had been cut off. Only Brit remained—a brown moth of a Brit, very little different, she thought ruefully, from what she was now. She wondered why on earth Link had kept it. She shrugged and began looking around again.

There was a study positively bursting with books. That, she knew wisely, must be left strictly alone. There was a large dining-cum-lounge room, a small compact kitchen. There was only one bedroom.

She had reached the bedroom now, tan and brown as the rest of the apartment, and was mentally adding some soft yellow, perhaps some nasturtium to provide the colour that a woman must have, when he spoke from the doorway. She had not heard him knock to be let in, but she presumed that when he had deposited her here while he checked up on the office he had taken a key. Anyway, he stood there.

'Do you think it will do until we can find something larger?' he asked. 'Perhaps build our own roof tree?'

'It's an excellent bachelor flat' she conceded, 'but a little confined for more than one.'

'Not when you're in love,' he said tauntingly. 'Even a single bed is ample when love sleeps there as well.'

Aware of her reddened cheeks, she remarked: 'Most flats are now two-bedroom units.'

'One room is enough.' Again he said it tauntingly, and she knew he was laughing at her.

'Go ahead with any redecoration, any colour alteration,' he tossed. 'Although we won't be here long we might as well be happy as any wall wash will give us.'

'I like the colour. I like the autumn shades.'

'Good. Everything else suit you?'

'Not,' Brit said, 'the out-of-date photograph.'

'Which one?'

'Are there more?'

'No. Only you. So you don't like it?'

'No.'

'All the same it remains, Mrs. Wayland.'

'Why?'

'It's a long story. I'll tell you one day. But meanwhile don't dare lay a finger on it. Understand?'

'I think I do. I think it's there to remind you what I was like when you bought me.'

'Go on.'

'Though why,' she said desperately, 'why you ever bought me is beyond understanding.'

'That's another story I'll tell you one day.'

'One thing,' Brit sighed. 'I haven't altered. I'm still Father's brown moth.'

'Your father,' he shrugged, 'was a fool.'

She turned angrily on him, but he spoke before she could.

'No, he wasn't a fool, he was too shrewd for a fool.'

'Can my family be left out of this?'

'All your family can,' he came back.

That brought Cara into Brit's mind, Cara who had still not written.

'She'll be all right,' Link said irritably when she spoke of Cara aloud.

'It's weeks. You'd think she would have scribbled a

note. Or . . .' a biting of Brit's lip . . . 'that John would.'

She was turned away from Link, but even turned away she felt, if she did not see, his sharp whirl round. But he said nothing.

'Go ahead,' he directed of the suite again, 'do anything you want to. Buy anything.'

'As you buy anything that catches your interest?'

'Meaning?'

'Nothing.'

'*Meaning*, Brit?' He started walking towards her.

Suddenly angry, not knowing why she should be, she flung: 'Well, you bought me, didn't you? That photo—'

'What about it?'

'It's a record, isn't it, a record of the first day of your purchase.'

'Actually,' he came in coldly, 'I had seen you before that. But yes, you're right, I had told the school board just around that time.'

'Why?'

'Because a school board has to be referred to, of course.'

'You know what I mean,' she insisted.

'I do. You mean why did I pick you? Good lord, don't you think I often ask that myself?'

'Link——'

'I ask myself why in hell and tarnation did I look a second time at—at——'

'At a nincompoop, an idiot, an oaf, a nong——'

'Brit,' he said with maddening triumph, 'you *do* listen to me!'

'You—you——' She could say no more. She flung herself angrily into the next room, expecting him, with his taunting tongue, to follow.

He didn't. He went out. She heard the door shut.

And with it, as often happened, and it dismayed her, she knew a curious disappointment, an anti-climax to something that hadn't happened ... and she wished had.

She wished had?—Oh, heavens, Brit thought, I can't, I don't, I mustn't feel like that for that man.

Yet 'that man' was her husband. If she had had any unreality about it during the day, Brit had none at night. On their wedding evening he had said: 'John. The nice gentleman. Ghosts, all of them.'

And, remembered Brit, they had been. There had been no man between herself and Link. She shivered a little and made herself concentrate on the room.

She had not gone to the arcade salon. Why should she? There had only been Simeon really to take her there. She had liked the girls, but that was all it had been, just a liking.

She was a little surprised then when Hilary Malling rang her.

'Mrs. Wayland, we thought you'd be round.'

'Why?' Brit started to ask, then stopped herself. It sounded a little insensitive.

'It would be very hard,' she said instead. 'As it must be for you.'

'For all of us. He was a fine person. We all loved Simeon.'

'Yes.'

'Please, won't you come? After all, you should take an interest.'

Should I? thought Brit. But why? I liked Simeon, I liked him very much, but why should I——

'We, the girls and I, would like to see you. Later when some of the shock is over, do come round.'

'Yes,' Brit heard herself say. She put down the phone.

She absorbed herself in the redecoration, putting

more into it than she felt actually, for after all it was only a place of bricks and mortar, but at least it was something to do.

She finished the sole bedroom ... 'one room is enough', he had said ... then went to the lounge. She was pleased with the result, so pleased that she determined to tackle the study. She knew that a study was sacrosanct, but she still felt she could make something more of it than the brown enclosure it was now. If she was careful not to move a book, disarray a paper, Link might not mind her adding a touch here and there. If it came alive, as she pictured it coming alive, he might even appreciate her work. And suddenly Brit knew she wanted Link's appreciation. She wanted his praise. She wanted to glow in that praise.

I am that fool, nincompoop, oaf, she thought in surprise.

She changed the carpet to a warmer colour. She added a big black leather chair. The straight-hanging curtains were exchanged for tie-backs to let in more natural light. As a last thought she bought and placed a silver calendar on the desk.

Placing it into position, Brit disarranged Link's large green blotter. She straightened it to how he had had it before, then saw that the movement had disengaged a letter evidently pushed into the under leather flap.

She put the letter back.

Brit had gone on to something else ... in fact it all could have been a movie double-take ... when the significance of the name of the addressee on the letter came to her.

Miss B. Smith. For several moments that meant nothing; she had become accustomed now to Mrs.

Wayland. Then—Miss B. Smith. She was . . . had been . . . that.

She went back and took the letter out. It was addressed to the flat, their old flat, so it must be hers. But how was it that she never had received it?

Then she remembered how Link had established her in the hotel. It must have come after her departure, and the landlord either sent it on or Link collected it himself. But if he had, why hadn't he given it to her?

She looked at the date. It had arrived before her marriage with Link, barely arrived, but it had still come before.

Had Link forgotten it, at a time like that you were likely to forget anything, but if so had he kept on forgetting afterwards? He was an extremely cool man, he had everything in control always, she thought it unlikely that Link would forget.

In her absorption she did not hear him come in. She had been expecting him, and had looked forward to his pleased surprise, for the room did look nice.

But all he did was stand at the door and look at Brit looking at the letter.

'Been snooping?'

'I have not.'

'Anyway, you've found it, haven't you?'

'Found what?'

'Found what you hold in your hand.'

'Had it been lost?' she asked.

'Not lost, concealed. I never expected you to come in here.'

'I know. I know studies are personal places——'

'Then why in tarnation did you intrude?'

She could have understood it if she had not been on the right side. Holding a letter addressed to yourself, a letter that never had been passed on, must make hers the right side.

'Did you forget to give me this?' she asked.

'No.'

'You mean—you withheld it deliberately?'

'Yes.'

'How dared you? Just how dared you, Link?'

'It came shortly before our marriage. I was letting nothing get in the way of that marriage. I didn't know what was in the letter, I didn't know who had written it, but I wasn't taking a chance.'

'You're abominable!' she burst out.

'Yes,' he agreed. 'Well,' he went on after a moment, 'aren't you going to open John's letter?'

'I wouldn't know whose letter it was.' He smiled thinly, and she said a little wildly: 'I've never had a letter from John.'

'Only written to him.'

'Nor that, either, though it's no business of yours.'

'It was no business,' Link said. 'It is now.'

'Whoever wrote this letter' ... Brit was turning the letter over ... 'wrote it before it was your business.' She looked at the man. 'Why have I only got the letter now?'

'I forgot it,' he admitted.

'In the past weeks, perhaps, but when you actually received it?'

'Then,' he admitted coolly, 'I simply withheld it.'

'You *what*?'

'I withheld it. I thought it might be John's, and I wanted nothing to upset my plans, I wanted no man standing between my bride and me. After that' ... he shrugged ... 'I really forgot.' He added: 'You can believe that or not.'

'I believe nothing from you,' she cried. She looked down again at the letter, the letter with that telltale date. She looked at the stamp. It had been posted at——

'Open it,' Link said. 'Don't tease yourself.'

'It's waited this long, it can wait longer.'

'Open it, Brit.'

'I'll open it when I please, and I don't please now.'

'You'll damn well get this thing over. Either that or I'll open it for you myself. Read it out.'

'You dare!'

'I mean it, Brit. Open it, I say.'

She saw his angry eyes, his hard lips, she saw his half step forward. She opened the letter.

'Is it from——' he asked.

'Yes. John.'

She said it dully. She was reading the letter, reading at first with joy, then with frustration, then with anger, but anger at Link, never John.

'My dear,' John had written, 'my very very dear, my darling, darling Brit. Can you forgive me for not being in touch at once? But I wanted to be sure of what I could offer you before I spoke out, before I told you what I've never told you—but have felt. I think, I pray, we both have felt.

'When only Cara met me on the plane when I had expected you and Cara ... yes, that's so, that's what she'd told me ... I was nearly out of my mind. But it was too late. We'd left by then. Later Cara admitted to me what she had written to you ... that crazy marriage story. She did it, she said, to make sure you would make no move to stop her, but I really think she meant it so you would make no move to retrieve, or try to retrieve, any of the money. I was dumbfounded, Brit, so much so I could think of nothing, do nothing. When later I did regain my senses I knew how wonderful it would be if I could tell you of my success when I wrote about Cara's deception, tell you that any monetary loss you had sustained was now inconsequential.

'Well, dear Brit, I *am* telling you, telling you that *Southern Cross* has been accepted, that I am on the up-grade at last—But telling you most of all that I love you. Brit, I love you. As soon as I can I'm coming. Coming home to my girl.

'Always—Your John.'

CHAPTER TWELVE

BRIT could not have said how long she stood there looking at the letter, John's letter; she could not have said how long she still would have stood had Link not called to her.

'Are you sharing it?' he asked harshly, and the roughness stiffened her.

'No,' she said.

'I could take it from you, you know that.'

'Oh, I know it' ... bitterly ... 'you can take anything you want. You have the means to buy it, and if it's beyond cost, you have the brute strength.'

'Wouldn't strength do without the brute?'

'No,' she said tonelessly.

He was rolling his cigarette, that old ritual once more. She turned away as he licked the edges of the paper together, for some reason she could never bear to watch Link do that.

'It's all right,' he said cursorily, 'I've finished.' Brit flushed vividly. Why did this man always know? she thought.

'I suppose a gentleman would withdraw quietly,' Link said, 'leave you to read it again. Only' ... a pause ... 'I'm not a gentleman. Tell me what it contains, Brit.'

'I won't.'

'In that case I'll have the letter.' He actually began to cross to her.

'No,' she said. Then she amended: 'If I tell you, will that do?'

'You mean cut the love and kisses?'

'John might not be a writer, but he's not as banal as that.'

'Give me the general trend.' His voice was harsh again.

'It was all a lie about John and Cara,' Brit reported dully. 'Cara had told John we both would be on his plane, supposedly surprising him. He had expected us.'

'Why should Cara do that?'

'It would make the marriage part more convincing to me, I expect, two on a plane together.'

'You mean' ... a pause ... 'that that's the lie you're talking about?'

'Yes.'

'That he didn't intend marrying her?'

'No.'

'But he did intend marrying you?'

'In time. If he made a success.'

'And this letter says he has?'

'Yes.'

The silence was a long one this time. When Link spoke it was about Cara once more. 'Why did that archdemoness tell such a story?'

'She needed the money, I suppose, *all* the money. By involving John in the way she did, she knew I would be too wretched to do anything.'

'I see. A bright little button, that sister of yours.'

'Oh, Cara's bright,' Brit said.

'The thing that bugs me is why your swain didn't get in touch at once. Why didn't he come back? At least why didn't he cable?'

'He wanted to be a success. He was only thinking of me.'

'Well, take it like that if you want to, but in my book it suggests a laggard lover.'

'John is not!' she said hotly.

'Laggard is one who loiters behind the others, or'—significantly—'the other. Singular. You could say a come-late. My dear Brit, your John was a come-late.'

'Yes. You saw to that,' said Brit.

'I saw to it because I had made my plans and there was a chance the letter could delay them.'

'Delay!' she said in contempt. As though John's letter would only 'delay.' Why, it would put END to it all.

'I think you're trying to tell me that it would be something stronger than delay,' Link came in. 'In which case I'm glad I did what I did.'

She looked at him curiously ... and, though she was unaware of it, a little piteously. Why was this man always so brutal? He had had a bad childhood, but surely he had stepped away from that now. He wanted something better for himself than his parents had had, he had said so, but you don't reap a harvest from hard dry ground. Link, she almost called out, take off your armour, or at least show me a chink in the metal. Yet what did she want even with a softer Link? She had nothing for him. It was John, it always had been John. Simeon she had liked very much, she had wanted somehow to protect him, but John—What did it matter then how hard was this man?

'That's all you have to tell, then?' He said it almost disinterestedly. 'No plans for the future. That is' ... a thin smile ... 'on the laggard lover's part?'

'There was a plan. He was coming home to marry me.'

'Too bad.' It was almost drawled. Picking up a sheaf of papers, Link went casually out.

Suddenly Brit wanted to run after him, face him, tell him what she thought of him. Slap that unsmiling-smiling face.

Only, she knew, I would be slapped back.

She began mechanically on the room again, and as she worked, she worked, too, on a reply to John.

... 'John, if only you had written earlier ...'

... 'John, why didn't you tell me at once?'

But when she wrote that night all Brit said was:

'I'm married to Link Wayland, John. Can you tell me about Cara? Should you meet her tell her to write. Tell her the episode is over.'

She had added: 'You and I are over, too.' Then she had signed it simply: 'Brit.'

Link commended her work on the apartment. 'You certainly have a touch. Though of course the unlimited resources helped. Do you think you could have done as well on John's stint?'

'It's not a stint!' she snapped.

'It is also not Wayland weight.'

'Wayland, Wayland, Wayland!'

'Yes, Mrs. Wayland,' Link smiled. 'Tell me,' he said once, 'if I'd delivered the letter in time would you have——'

She had turned fully on him. 'Yes, Link, I would.'

'Would have waited for John or would have gone through with it?'

'I would never have gone through with it.' She said it coolly and deliberately and unmistakably, and she wondered how she could speak like that when inside of her there was a hot turmoil, no cool deliberation at all.

The next day he told her to have a divan put in his study. He said: 'I can't sleep with ghosts.'

'But you're the one who said there would be no one between,' she reminded him, wondering why she did.

'Put it this way' ... the dry whisper of the tobacco in his big palm again ... 'I'm older and wiser.'

'Link, I'm not a child, I'm aware that as a wife it's my duty——'

'My God, Brit, you know how to be cruel, don't you? Duty.' He stood looking down at her for a long moment. Then: 'Get that divan put in,' he ordered.

A week went past. Two weeks. A letter came from John.

It was nostalgic, it was wistful, longing, regretful. Whether it had acceptance or not, Brit could not have told. She read it again and again, but she still did not know, yet John must have accepted, she decided, for he asked nothing more of her. The excitement of his success was helping him, she thought. He said that he would stay on a while yet in Europe. The company had asked him to, and he had declined before, but now—He hoped Brit was happy, then left it at that. Then he said:

'Cara has gone to England to try her luck there. She's good, Brit, but there are dozens as good. Many better. I'm sorry if that upsets you, but it's well for someone to know the truth. To be frank I don't think Cara was cut out for a dancer, there are more than dreams in her pretty little head. At a rough guess I would say business would be her forte. Your father should have had her taught book-keeping instead.'

Brit left the letter around. She wanted Link to ask her about it. She wanted to tell him that everything was finished ... she wanted to tell him quite desperately. But he didn't ask, so Brit did not tell.

She went out to see the girls at Simeon's and was surprised at the way they greeted her, just as if they had expected her to come, as though she belonged there. Hilary Malling even asked her advice over an order. When she left they wanted to know when she would be there again. Brit was puzzled, but she did not think much about it. *Then.*

But she thought about it that night.

Link was busy, had been busy for a week. He had told Brit that while the rush was on he would be eating in town. He was also sleeping more nights than not in the city hotel suite that he kept for himself or for overseas visitors, for most mornings Brit found the study bed had not been disturbed.

Brit had become used to it. In Link's present mood she had preferred it. When she reached the apartment tonight and saw his car and realized he was there, she felt first of all a swift gladness that she would not be alone, but followed at once by a nervous uneasiness. The car was untidily parked, not the way Link usually did things. He must have been in a hurry to run up the stairs, she thought.

She went up the stairs herself. She unlocked the door and went into the apartment. Link was standing at the bar he had had installed, and he had a stiff whisky in his hand. When he looked across at her she knew by the careless way he held the glass that there had been glasses before this one.

'Home from business, eh?' he greeted her.

She looked at him, confused.

'Home from Brit's, late Simeon's,' he went on. 'Or will you keep the old name?'

She still stared at him, then, when he did not enlighten her, she said: 'Yes, I have been to see the girls.'

'Your girls.'

'Simeon's,' she corrected.

'Now Brit's. Or' ... he repeated his prior question ... 'will you keep the old name?'

'Link, what on earth are you talking about?'

Link said deliberately: 'I'm talking about your

little concern, Brit, your arcade boutique, salon, whatever you choose to call it.'

'It's not mine. Simply because I go out to see Hilary and——'

'It *is* yours,' he said harshly. 'Don't lie to me, Mrs. Wayland. You know as well as I know ... *now* ... what Simeon did with his worldly goods.'

'You're mad!' she gasped.

'Yes, mad to have believed you when you put up that pretence of not wanting to meet him over in Hawaii.—"I'd sooner be alone," you said when I told you that you were to have a companion while I flew over to L.A. "I'm perfectly safe." Then: "I might take a dislike to him."' Link gave a short ugly laugh. He poured himself another whisky.

'Then when I returned from Los Angeles and asked you how you found him it was—"Oh—— he was nice" in an uninterested tone of voice. Tell me' ... putting down the whisky and crossing to take Brit's wrist in a hurting grip ... 'whom was the uninterest for? Me? To put me off the scent? Or that poor wretch now that you'd got what you wanted out of him?'

She tugged her wrist away. Leaning up, she caught him a blow across his cheek, but only a single blow. He grabbed her arm away and warned: 'Do that again, Brit, and by heaven you'll have it done to you.'

'You shouldn't have said that,' she muttered.

'But you did pretend uninterest, you did give the impression you had never met him. Admit it, Brit.'

She was silent a moment, then she said in a low voice: 'Yes, I did that.'

'V to M?' he asked. 'No, not view to matrimony, it was too late for that, but view to money, more of.'

'No.'

'Then why, for heaven's sake? Don't tell me you fell

in love with him?'

'I liked him very much.'

'I said love.'

'Why shouldn't I love him?' she demanded.

'He is ... was ... not your type. He was a very good person, I would say, no devious undercurrents like Mrs. Wayland.'

'Don't call me that!'

'But I can hardly call you Miss Smith,' he reminded her brutally. 'Not—now.' His eyes flicked remindingly at her.

She started to turn away, then turned back. This was something that had to be cleared up now.

'Link,' she appealed, 'will you please tell me? It may seem that I know, but I assure you I don't.'

'It takes a lot of believing, Brit,' he answered seriously.

'Then believe.'

He was silent a moment. 'Even if I do believe you,' he said presently, 'even if you knew nothing of the bequest, as you assert, you still can't deny your lies and evasions.'

'You mean giving you the impression that I hadn't met Simeon?'

'I mean that. Why, Brit?'

Why? There had been nothing to hide and yet she had not told him. But Simeon, too, had withheld from Link the fact that he had already met Link's wife. 'I like him so much,' Simeon had said, 'that I wouldn't want him hurt.'

But Brit could not say that because she did not like Link. No ... *no* ... and the sudden realization came so sharply, so poignantly that instinctively she put out her hand to the back of a chair to steady herself ... I don't like Link.

I love him.

'Brit, are you all right?' Link's voice seemed to come from a distance. She saw him looking anxiously at her. 'Damned if I don't have to believe you when you say you knew nothing about Simeon's will,' he went on, 'for you certainly seem surprised enough. But you still have to answer for your pretence to me. For heaven's sake tell me, Brit, tell me why you made me think you didn't know the man.'

Why? Why again? But this time Brit knew the answer, an answer that was too unbelievable ... and yet it was true. She had pretended to Link not because she had been afraid of losing him. Because even then, though she hadn't known it, she had loved him. Loved Link Wayland! Loved the roughrider!

'Don't stand there concocting more lies.' His voice came in angrily. 'My God, Brit, have you no conscience at all?'

It was a splash of cold water. Brit felt herself recovering. She looked at Link. He didn't love her, he possessed her. Never once in their union had he said 'I love you' because he was not interested in love, only in possession. He would not be interested now.

She heard herself say coolly: 'I'd like confirmation of all this.'

'Guthrie and Fenton are the law men. By some coincidence my solicitors, too.'

'But aren't wills a private affair?' Her voice was cold. She felt herself shivering, yet not from any chill but from what she had just discovered about herself. She looked at him obliquely, knowing he would put a different interpretation on that chilly note. He would deduce from it that she was questioning his pre-knowledge of the affair.

He did deduce just that. He said: 'Yes. Private.

But then so is marriage. Guthrie and Fenton naturally thought that being your husband I was entitled to know.'

'Before I knew?'

'They're an old-fashioned firm,' Link shrugged. 'They still believe the male is the head of the house.'

'Can I see the will?' she asked.

'You'll have to see it,' he said brusquely. 'You'll have to sign a lot of papers, have to prove that you're indeed that legatee. But if it's so urgent right now I think I can tell you what you will read. I would say it would be: '...to my friend, Brit Wayland, I give, devise and bequeath——'

He did not finish, or if he did Brit did not hear him. She had run from the room, from the flat, from the apartment block. She did not stop until she reached the street.

Brit walked for miles. She walked until it was dark. '... to my friend, Brit Wayland, I give, devise and bequeath——' She heard Link taunting her with it again. Simeon's will. Simeon's last wish. '... to Brit Wayland, I give, devise and bequeath——' And Link firmly believed if she had not exactly contrived this, then at least she had done nothing to avoid it.

Like failing, for instance, to tell Link in Hawaii that she knew Simeon already. Like merely telling Link after the tragedy that Simeon was 'nice.'

Link was right, everything he had said of her had been true. Except the motive. Except the feeling. For the feeling she had had for Simeon had only been a gentle one, there had been nothing there apart from that. She truly believed there had been nothing either on Simeon's side for all that he had said he loved her. Only a very deep gratefulness for her friendship. So deep, it now turned out, that he had made her his legatee. Oh, Simeon, Brit grieved, you were too young to die yet.

Little things came back to her as she walked along the darkling streets. People were coming home from work, as she had come once. Those days seemed a million years ago now. So much had happened since. She recalled Simeon standing at the crater Haleakala, House of the Sun. She had been nervous, but Simeon had been engrossed. He had said: 'I felt at peace. I felt strong, Brit.' Simeon who obviously had not been strong.

Then later, on that beautiful tinsel Hawaiian night, he had told her he had no one. When she lightly answered that sometimes one was better off, he had replied: 'That was to explain to you what I've done.'

Finally, when he had been dying, he had looked up and said two words. 'For you.' He had meant what he had willed to her.

Oh, Simeon, Simeon! Brit began to cry.

Because, even in an uncaring homebound throng, tears are noticed, Brit went home, too. She was relieved to see Link's car gone.

She did not go out the next day. Link did not come. It was the same the day after, except that a cheque arrived from her husband, presumably to feed and clothe her, she thought with rising anger. How dared Link, how dared he treat her like this without letting her speak first? Oh, yes, he had heard her out, but had he *listened*? Did that roughrider of a man ever listen to any other voice but his own?

The third day the letter from the solicitors arrived. It told Brit what Link Wayland already had told her, that she had inherited Simeon's. She was asked to come to their office.

She left it several days and during those days another cheque arrived from Link. What did he think she did with his wretched money? Eat it? Make paper dolls of it? Even the first cheque was untouched as yet.

She rang and made an appointment with Guthrie and Fenton. The firm, as Link had said, proved an old-fashioned one.

Brit, on edge, still not believing what had happened, said pointedly: 'Mr. Wayland acquainted me with all this before you did.'

Old Mr. Guthrie smiled paternally and answered: 'As he is your husband, my dear, we thought that would be right.'

It wasn't right, Brit felt like retorting, like wiping that kind of look off Mr. Guthrie's amiable married face. Because, she would have liked to say, not all marriages are kind and amiable. Ours isn't. But the senior solicitor was reading what Link already had told her. 'I give, devise and bequeath ...'

She barely listened. She barely listened when Mr. Guthrie told her that the bequest was the salon only, that any moneys had been otherwise accounted for. He advised Brit very strongly to go to the salon, spend some time there.

'For,' he finished cautiously, 'every business has two economic sides, Mrs. Wayland, the side to the customer, the side to the owner. Not always is the owner's side what the customer, or public, might think.'

Brit nodded. She signed papers. Finally she got up, shook Mr. Guthrie's hand and left.

It was a week since she had seen Link. She wondered what he would do if she suddenly turned up at his office.

She didn't, of course, she went home, and there awaited a third cheque.

It was just too much. Brit collected the others and put them all under a paperweight in his study. At some time or other she estimated he must come and see them. But he would not see her. She would not be here.

She packed her bag. She was recalling a small residential not far from Simeon's. She had walked past it a dozen times, and its Vacancy notice was clear in her mind. It would do for a while.

She left no note. She simply walked out. But before she shut the door behind her, she looked around. Their first home, you could almost say, only a small one, but——

'One room is enough,' Link had said. 'Even a single bed is ample when love sleeps there as well.'

Love?

Brit closed the door.

CHAPTER THIRTEEN

THE room was drab. The apartment Brit and Cara had shared had been anything but a luxury one, but at least they had had their possessions strewn around—Cara's absurd dolls that she collected, Brit's favourite prints. This place had nothing.

But Brit considered she was lucky to have obtained a corner to sleep in so easily, though probably the drabness had seen to that. As soon as she had unpacked, she went down and bought a cheap meal, cheap because after she had paid the proprietor, who had insisted on settlement in advance, there had been very little left. Little, anyway, when you had to consider all the tomorrows.

Brit smiled rather crookedly when she thought of those big cheques waiting in Link's study. They would have paid for her room here for several months. For her meals, and not cheap ones. As to any other money—well, she simply hadn't handled any. Link had bought everything for her, bought too much, she had needed nothing. But when it came to actual money ... All she possessed now were a few American dollars left over from Hawaii that she had changed into Australian currency. That was all. Well, not to worry, she was the owner of Simeon's now, and tomorrow she must present herself there as the owner, not as she had presented herself before, as someone simply visiting the girls. She felt herself withdrawing nervously at the thought. How would they consider her? They had been Simeon's old and trusted employees; she was someone who had just come in at the end. Yet were they unaware? She recalled the way that they had greeted her, as though they had expected her to come. Hilary had said: '... after all, you should take an interest.' It had puzzled her.

But she understood now ... though if that made her wiser it did not make her happier. It had been all right, her thoughts ran wretchedly on, when she hadn't known what Simeon had done, but now that she was aware of her position, it was an ordeal. She wished desperately she did not have to go on.

Still, short of having the solicitors sell the place, she must comply, and certainly she must if she intended to carry on, and Brit did intend that. What else, she thought, do I have? She wished she could feel enthusiastic over it. It would be wonderful to hide oneself in work, forget everything else like career women seemed to do. Only, knew Brit, a career woman I am *not*. Any interest I have in the executive side will have to be forced. I am what Father always said: a brown moth.

She went to sleep at last on the rather uncomfortable bed on that discouraging note.

She timed her arrival for mid-morning. If she had turned up earlier, she thought sensitively, it could have looked as though she had come to claim what now belonged to her.

She had awakened hours ago, but had laid in the narrow bed staring at the drab room until she estimated the shop where she had bought her cheap dinner last night would be open for breakfast. She had washed in a discouraging bathroom along the passage, dressed, then gone downstairs. The proprietor had asked would she be stopping another night, and when she said yes, reminded her that all rooms must be paid for in advance. After she had paid, Brit estimated that breakfast must be very meagre since there were more breakfasts for other mornings to be bought.

She had sat over tea and toast for as long as she could, then spent several hours in the park. A family on the next bench sat eating from a bag of buns, and Brit thought ruefully that she could have eaten a bun, too. For an heiress ... she was that, she supposed, in a way ... she was in a decidedly bad monetary position. Yet if I have a bun, she thought, not far from hysterical laughter, I'll have to buy that much less lunch.

She looked at her watch, and estimated she could now walk round to the arcade.

With every step she grew more nervous. She could see Hilary Malling looking a little scornfully on her. All the girls darting her slightly contemptuous looks. And why not? In their books she was a newcomer, a Johnny-Come-Lately, female version, someone who had manoeuvred her way into Simeon's life, a life that had stopped soon after. Very convenient for the one to whom he had slanted his will, they could think.

'Mrs. Wayland ... Brit!' There was no doubting the warmth in Hilary Malling's voice as she came out of the arcade to greet Brit even before Brit entered the boutique. The rest of the staff smiled welcomingly at her. Hilary made coffee at once, and they drank it in the room where Simeon had dreamed up his designs.

'Thank heaven you've come,' the head assistant said. 'This ship badly needs a helmsman.' She smiled and corrected, 'Helmswoman.'

'But I'm not. I mean ... Oh, Hilary, I didn't know anything about any of this. Can—can you believe that?'

'About the salon? Of course you didn't. But I did, and I believe the girls guessed.'

'But how? But why?'

'It's simple really. Simeon wanted you to have it. Just

as simple as that.'

'But why?' Brit asked again.

Hilary poured more coffee, took her time in creaming and sugaring it.

'Didn't the solicitor explain anything?' she asked.

'Only that I inherited the salon. Oh' ... remembering ... 'he did say that Simeon's money had been accounted for.'

'Exactly. Simeon wasn't rich, Brit, very far from it, but he did have a comfortable, if decidedly less than large, amount. Which' ... looking quizzically at Brit ... 'he divided entirely between the staff.'

'Oh, I'm glad to hear that,' Brit said wholeheartedly.

Hilary heaved a sigh of relief. 'Then I ... we ... are certainly glad to hear you say that. So many legatees could be resentful, could wonder why they hadn't received that very necessary cash.'

'Necessary?' queried Brit.

'It is neccessary,' nodded Hilary, 'because businesswise this salon is by no means a goldmine. Never was. It was entirely because of Simeon.' Her face grew soft. 'We have a lot of outstanding debts, Brit.'

'Tell me everything, Hilary,' Brit begged.

'All of us here started with Simeon,' Hilary complied. 'Everyone of us stayed. We also would have stayed. Simeon was that kind of person.'

'Yes, he was,' agreed Brit.

'Simeon was exceptional. His gift had to be recognized, and it was. But being recognized doesn't always bring in the money, Brit; also Simeon would never make do, he had to have the best. To be a financially successful house you have to be careful here and there. In a lining, perhaps, or a button, or a cheaper thread. But never Simeon. Also, many of his designs were beautiful but not—well, not called-for. He would not bow to demand, he only followed his instincts, and they were exceptional but not always acceptable. When you go through Simeon's desk you'll find dozens of glorious sketches, dresses that elegant countesses would buy, but where in Australia' ... Hilary made a rueful moue ... 'do you meet elegant countesses?'

'I see what you mean.'

'There is a wonderful business here ... but not exactly the kind of business Simeon dreamed of. There have to be practicalities as well as dreams. And that, I'm afraid, will be your job, Brit.'

'Yet why me?' Brit looked at the older woman with frank eyes. 'I don't know how you and the girls consider me, Hilary, but never at any time were Simeon and I ... were we ... I mean ...' She flushed and broke off.

Hilary leaned over and took Brit's hand. 'We know just how Simeon felt about you, Brit. Remember we'd all been together right from the concept, we knew each other like brother and sister. Remember, too, that Simeon left *us*, not *you*, his money. But he left you what he *loved*, Brit—the salon. He left it because he loved you.'

'But I didn't——'

'We know that, too. Simeon knew. He knew how you felt about your husband.'

Brit bit her lip. If Simeon had known, then it must have been remarkable intuition, for she herself had not known. Not then. Why, she remembered, she had even told Simeon on that first day in his boutique that it was not a 'special' wedding. He had understood what she had meant.

'I still can't understand,' Brit said presently. 'There must have been something else.'

'There was. Simeon was not strong. But I suppose

you sensed that?'

'Yes, I did.'

'If it hadn't happened as it has, then it would have happened fairly soon in some other way. He knew it. We did. And he had no relations.'

'He had his good friends,' said Brit, 'he had them in his employees.'

'But not one of them with capital,' Hilary insinuated. 'Simeon knew you had that. He believed that if ... when ... it came to it, when he had to go, you could carry on. Employ the staff he already employed.' Hilary gave a small sigh. 'He never stopped thinking of people. He remembered us.'

'No, he was everything dear,' agreed Brit wretchedly. 'But he was also very wrong.'

Hilary looked questioningly at her.

'You see, I have no money,' Brit explained.

'But——'

'My husband has it, yes, but that's not me.'

'I've met Mr. Wayland,' said Hilary. 'He seemed to me to be the kind of person who would like to have a finger in all kinds of pies. I know from the papers it's not just the news world with him.'

'He would like it. But it would have to be his finger only in the pie. Oh' ... impatiently ... 'why talk in circles? The fact is, Hilary, I've left him. I don't want his money, I hate his money. I also' ... deliberately ... 'don't want him.'

'Brit ... Mrs. Wayland ...' Hilary began.

'I would sooner Brit, and if you're going to say: "Are you sure?" then yes, I am sure. So' ... a shrug ... 'I just have to make this work by myself, don't I?'

'Yes,' Hilary Malling agreed. But there was a small doubt in her voice. Presently she said: 'I'll leave you to go through Simeon's things.'

Brit cried a little over Simeon's dreams, for that was what she called the piles of scraps of sketches pushed in his office pigeonholes. A girl reaching to pluck a blossom from a tree and the folds of her dress following her fluid movement. A girl on a hilltop with a wind blowing silken skirts so that the skirts became part of the wind itself. Oh, yes, Simeon had had a rare talent.

She was still sitting absorbed when Hilary brought in a lunch tray. The older woman's eyes fell on the picture that Brit was studying now, for all Simeon's designs were that, they were more artistry than pattern. This time Simeon's model held a basket of oranges, and the lines of the frock were equally softly rounded as the globes of golden fruit.

Hilary half sighed. Brit looked up at her. Now she knew she understood. 'Too beautiful?' she asked.

'Yes. That is if a thing can be that. You see, Brit, to keep this place going there had to be less of the fine seams and more of the—the—well, you know what I mean.'

'Yes, I know,' Brit said regretfully, putting away Simeon's last design. When Hilary had gone, she closed the desk. Closed up Simeon's dreams, she thought.

'Good-bye, my dear,' she said softly.

Brit found cheaper lodgings. The room she had obtained when she had left Link had been poor enough, but it had functioned on a daily basis. This bedsitter was weekly, so more moderate still. It also gave Brit more scope to add a personal touch or two, make it a little less barren. Though very little, she thought ruefully, surveying it in the week-end after a day's toil on it, with nothing to work on, or work with, all she could hope to do with it was to make it not so much of a cell.

She had not heard from Link, but she had not expected to. She had read in the paper that he was making a flying visit to London. Probably he had gone without returning to the flat. If he had rung he would have thought that she was out, or refusing to answer. He would not have seen the untouched cheques. She supposed there would be more cheques again poked under the door by the mailman. She had not stopped the mail.

She could have done with those cheques now. She thought that rather desperately when the accounts came in.

'The trouble is,' Hilary said tactfully when shown the accounts, 'you're buying the wrong way.' She added: 'As Simeon did.'

'Well, if Simeon did it——'

'Simeon did it because he hadn't the right kind of money to buy any other way.'

'Neither have I.'

'No,' agreed Hilary significantly. 'You see,' the head assistant went on after a pause, 'to buy more reasonably you must buy bigger.'

'We're not doing well enough for that,' said Brit.

This was true. Although people came and looked wistfully at the lovely things, because of the more expensive buying the goods were more expensive. It seemed a vicious circle.

'If only we could get a loan. It would be paid back in no time. There would be no risk,' Hilary said once again.

'I can't,' Brit answered in the same way as she had before.

At the end of the month when Brit went through the books as thoroughly as her rather less-than-financial brain could help her, she could see that for all her efforts, and she *had* tried, Hilary and all the girls had assured her of that, that Simeon's was not advancing. That a few more months of this could only end in one thing—closure.

The next day Link rang.

'Miss Smith?' His voice came carelessly over the wire—but Brit's heart was not careless, it thumped with almost painful deliberation.

'Brit Wayland here.' She knew he had said Smith intentionally and she made of it a prop to brace herself.

'I've just returned from New York,' he told her, ignoring her correction.

'The paper said London.'

'Oh, so you read me up?'

'I just happened to see the item.'

'I went to the flat for the first time since I walked out ... you walked out, too, apparently ... that last day. I found the cheques. What gives, Brit?'

'You don't,' she came crisply back. She commended herself mentally on that.

'Doing all right with Simeon's, then?' he asked.

'Thank you, yes,' she lied.

A pause at the other end, then:

'Well, I will say you're not like many girls – most, I would estimate. Even if they have enough there's always room for more. Money, I mean.'

'I have ample,' she assured him.

'Simeon did you well, eh?'

'I need nothing,' she said firmly.

'You mean—nothing from me?'

'Did you have anything else to say?'

'Yes. I was wondering if you forbid me sending you money if you also forbid me sending—something else?'

'I have everything—I told you.'

'Anyway, it's being sent, Brit, whether you forbid it or not. It comes with my best wishes. Do what you like with it, it's yours.' Link finished: 'With my blessing.'

'Link?' Brit called, puzzled, but his phone was down. What had he meant? she wondered.

As Brit was closing up that evening, John came in.

The staff had gone. If she could not promise them any future Brit had at least been determined that they enjoyed good conditions now. She always insisted that they got away promptly. If any stragglers came in, she attended to them. Why not? She had only a bedsitter to go home to.

Brit stood looking stupidly at John for a long minute. In the end it was John who came forward to take her hand in his.

'Brit!'

'I thought you were in Europe, John,' she whispered.

'I flew in last night.'

'Didn't things' ... Brit paused sensitively ... 'Didn't they come out as you planned?'

'More than I planned. I'm signed to do the theme music for a new thing they're starting. Something quite fresh, a new concept. I'm very excited about it, Brit.'

'That's wonderful. It's good to get what you want.'

There was a slight silence. Then John said meaningly: 'Not entirely what I want.'

'Oh, John!' she half laughed, half cried. But the cry was not for John.

'I came back here to wind up my affairs,' John said. 'It looks like I may be indefinitely in Europe, who knows? I may even be there for the rest of my life. One thing may lead to another. So' ... a hunch of his shoulders ... 'I'm shutting the door here.'

'And another door opening?'

'Yes. Brit' ... tentatively ... 'I wish we could go through that new door together.'

'It's too late,' she said flatly.

'It seems it ... but *is* it? I met your husband. He's quite a guy, isn't he?' ... Simeon had said that ... 'But would a man send another man, as Link Wayland did, to his wife? Because he did just that.' John looked bewildered. 'He sent me to you, Brit. Can you explain that to me?'

'Where did you meet?' she asked.

'I didn't know where to find you, so I went to Wayland's office. He was very decent to me, undoubtedly he's a very decent fellow, and that's what got me.'

'What, John?'

'He practically forced me to come here,' he explained.

'But you expressed a wish to see me?'

'Of course. But I thought he might suggest drinks together, all three of us, not—well——'

'What did Link say? I mean, how much did he tell you?'

John looked at her frankly. 'That things hadn't turned out, Brit. Then he said——' He paused.

'Yes?'

'He said to me: "It's your turn now."'

She was silent a moment. Link had said that!

'Then you came, John,' she half whispered.

'Yes.'

There was a long quiet in the boutique now. Shopping hours were over, only window gazers meandered through the arcade. The city traffic was becoming less busy, more muted. Brit looked at John across the room, but John, uncertain, still bemused, idly fingered a length of material and avoided Brit's gaze.

Presently he looked up again and said: 'It's not

what I came back for, Brit, this break-up of a marriage, I mean, and you must understand that.'

'You mean you didn't really come back for me?'

'No. How could I? I came back, as I said, to wind up my affairs here. When I called to see Wayland it was because I didn't want you to think I'd come and gone again without seeing you.' John let go the material and walked the narrow length of the boutique. 'But now it's different,' he said.

'Different?' she queried.

'You're not the married woman I thought you were.'

'I am married, John.'

'But not *the* married woman I believed. Brit, I would never have spoken like this had I thought for one moment that ... But it's not like that, is it? Anyway, Wayland has told me practically so himself. Besides, he's there, you're here. You don't even have the same address. So——'

'So, John?'

'So,' said John quietly, 'come with me, my dear.'

She did not answer at once. As unthinkingly as he had fingered the material, she picked up a dress, put it back on a hanger, did it all again.

'Why?' she asked at last.

'Because I love you. Because I believe you love me.'

'I don't think so. I mean, there was never anything *certain*, was there? We never spoke about it, never told each other. Why' ... a slight note of hysteria ... 'we never even kissed.'

'We looked across a room and knew. At least' ... eagerly ... 'I knew.'

'I believed I did, too—then. But——'

'Things don't change, Brit.'

'Sometimes they do.'

'You mean you love someone else?'

'I didn't say that.'

'But you meant it?'

'Oh, John, John,' was all Brit said. She went across to him and for the very first time he kissed her. When he had finished he gave her a little half-push away.

'That wasn't for me, was it?'

When she did not reply he went on: 'Not to worry—about me, I mean. I have my plate more than full. Too full, actually' ... a slight laugh ... 'for a loving wife as well. If it had happened, then I would have been apprehensive. A man can't have everything. As it is, I'm a lucky fellow. Shall we leave it at that?'

'You're dear, John,' she said softly.

'But not dear enough,' he teased ruefully. 'All right, Brit, the subject is closed. Unless you want me to report to Link Wayland and tell him it was no good.'

'No,' she said decisively, too decisively, 'don't do that.' He gave her a quick shrewd look, but he dropped the topic.

'You haven't asked me about your sister,' he said instead.

'You told me in your letter. You said she went to England. I wish' ... a little troubled ... 'Cara would write.'

'Probably thought she'd see you before any letter arrived.'

'What? What are you talking about, John?'

'Cara. She didn't go to England after all. I thought she had, then she turned up again. She'd changed her mind. Or' ... ruefully ... 'the money had run out.'

'She borrowed from you,' Brit said wretchedly. Was there nothing Cara would not do?

'I didn't mind, she's your sister, and I knew I wouldn't be seeing her again ... well, not for a long time.'

'With you both in Europe?'

'Both of us in Australia at the moment, though I won't be here long.'

Brit did not hear that, she was hearing only—'Both of us in Australia.'

'You mean Cara is back?' she demanded.

'Back, and, believe it or not, hanging back. I do believe for once that girl is ashamed.'

'Where is she? Where is she, John?'

'As a matter of fact, at the end of the arcade. I made her wait there, though it didn't take much making, she didn't want to come any more than I wanted her. Brit ... Brit!'

But Brit did not hear. She was running ... racing down the empty passage, calling her sister's name. She had no reason to run to her, but the heart has no reasoning, it simply loves.

'Cara!' she called, and Cara, standing waiting as John had said, turned and ran to her.

CHAPTER FOURTEEN

CARA's gentle humility lasted for exactly a month, and when the month was up Brit was almost glad. Quiet, chastened docility sat incongruously on Cara. The subdued mouse instead of the paradise bird was not her sister.

Tears had flowed. Cara had confessed everything, called herself every wretched creature in the universe, hung her head, thrown herself on Brit's mercy. That she meant it had been apparent when she even had not objected, vocally, anyway, to sharing Brit's mediocre bedsitter. After an involuntary 'Oh——' she had not said a word. She had even offered to make supper.

Over coffee she had asked tentatively about Link.

'When I heard through John,' she said, 'I thought how well you'd done for yourself. I mean' ... at a look in Brit's face ... 'I thought, I hope dear Brit is happy.'

That, Brit knew, Cara had *not* thought, or if she had it had been an afterthought. But it was no use trying to turn your back on Cara. Or close your heart. You could not, Brit knew, dictate to a heart.

'I'm sorry it didn't turn out.' Cara glanced quickly round the mean little room.

'Well, let's not talk about it. Let's talk about you, darling.'

'I didn't make it, Brit. To the top, I mean. Even halfway. Oh, I wasn't a flop, but—well——' Cara shrugged.

'John said there's a lot of competition.'

'Yes. And all of them ready to starve and grovel until

they get their foot on the ladder. Brit, I just couldn't, I'm not made that way. Anyhow' ... a slight sigh ... 'dancing is a bore.'

'But, Cara——'

'It was Daddy who insisted on it. Frankly I never liked it that much. I think the only part I did like was dressing up. I adore dressing.' Cara fiddled with her coffee spoon. 'What's this about you owning a boutique?'

Brit cut a short sigh. She was not in a mood to relate it to Cara, but she knew she must tell her some time. So she told.

Cara's eyes grew wide. 'A rich husband and a legacy as well!'

'Link and I have separated, and the legacy is a lovely but uneconomical dress salon that I haven't a hope of making prosper.'

'Can I see it, Brit?'

'Of course. Only——' Brit had been going to say 'Only don't get any ideas of taking over, for I'm wiser now.' She didn't say it, though, for the simple reason that Cara couldn't take over, not successfully. She had even less money than Brit, and Gowns by Simeon had to have capital.

'I'll come with you tomorrow, Brit,' Cara said eagerly.

'It would be better for you to look for a job.'

'Can't I work for you?'

'Cara, I have no money,' Brit pointed out.

'I'd work for nothing in a dress shop.'

'You still have to eat,' Brit reminded her. 'But don't let's discuss it now. You'll understand better when I show you Simeon's tomorrow.'

But Cara did not understand. She said so. She said: 'I can't understand anyone letting a place like this go.' She looked around her and her eyes were starry.

'It's not paying, Cara.'

'Make it.'

'That's easier to say than do.'

'*I* could do it.' Cara's voice trembled a little with excitement, but for all the slight shake there was a firm confidence there. A *knowledge*, you could say.

That was the first day.

Three weeks later, however hard Brit tried to turn away from the fact, deny it, refuse it, she still had to admit that Cara wasn't just efficient at business, she was excellent. She was even inspired. Discreetly at first, and then more boldly, Cara had stepped in and taken over a dozen things that Brit had been handling.—Or mishandling.

Ordering, for instance. Simeon's had never sold only their own dresses, they had bought from outside sources as well. Now Cara edged herself into the buying, ordered, then sold. Sold within days, hours.

'She has a talent,' Hilary said once to Brit during the second week.

Astonishingly ... astonishing to Brit ... Cara understood the books. She frowned over the clumsy balances Brit reached, and said: 'It's not good, yet not devastatingly bad, either. With decent capital——' She glanced obliquely at her sister.

'No, Cara.' Brit knew what Cara was thinking, or at least of whom Cara was thinking.

'No,' she said again.

Cara had left it at that ... *then*.

Though the staff did not actually like Cara—no girls ever liked her sister; Cara had had, Brit recalled, very few school friends—they still respected her get-up-and-go. Frankly that get-up-and-go astounded Brit; Cara always had been a lotus flower. Now she could not get to work quick enough.

It worried Brit. She was glad to see the boutique prosper ... for even in several weeks it had prospered ... but she did not know how long she could let Cara attend the salon, receiving for her services only her meals and a dress if it appealed to her. However, Cara seemed completely satisfied, to Brit's eyes, anyhow. It took Hilary Malling to open those eyes.

'Brit.' It was exactly a month now since Cara had returned. She was emerging from her chrysalis of contrition—Brit had seen the signs. She knew from Hilary Malling's voice that she was going to speak about her sister. She sighed. Cara could be very sharp if things did not suit her. She hoped she had not snapped at one of the girls. Now that her humility was gone that could be so.

She was not aware that she had said this aloud until Hilary said: 'Oh, no, they admire your sister tremendously. She's not you' ... an apologetic smile ... 'but perhaps that's better so far as they're concerned.'

Brit looked inquiringly at Hilary, and the senior assistant wasted no time.

'You're not a business woman, Brit.'

'I'm afraid that's true,' Brit admitted.

'Your sister, however, is born for trade.'

'Cara was born to be a dancer.'

'I don't think so. She doesn't think so, either.'

'Oh, I know she's got it into her head that she doesn't like dancing, but dancing *is* Cara.'

'It might have been, I don't know ... but I do know that dancing is not Miss Smith—*now*.'

'Then,' breathed Brit, 'what is?' But she knew she need not have asked. She knew the answer when it came would be one word and a proper name. It was. Hilary replied:

'Simeon's.'

'It can't be. For one thing my sister is not—well dependable,' Brit admitted wretchedly.

'You mean she *was* not. Perhaps that was because she was the wrong peg in the wrong hole. Now it's different.'

'For how long?'

'Does it matter? I mean so long as you can get Simeon's on its feet sufficiently even to sell it.'

'I don't want to sell it,' Brit said firmly.

'You want to keep on mismanaging it? Oh, I'm sorry, my dear, don't take this personally, but as the head of a concern you're about as good as dear Simeon was himself. Anyway, I didn't really mean that. About selling, Brit. All of the staff are very anxious that the salon remains. As you know, apart from sentimental interest, they all happen to be dependent on their jobs. I mentioned this before.'

'Yes, you did ... but, Hilary, how can I help?'

Hilary Malling took a deep breath.

'You could let Cara take over,' she said presently in a cautious voice.

'I don't mind doing that,' Brit admitted. 'I know I'm no good at it. But it doesn't solve the problem, does it? The problem of money, money that I don't happen to have.'

'Mr. Wayland has it.'

'No!'

'Then, Brit, you'll be closing the salon and putting a staff of worthwhile people ... you know yourself they're that ... out of work.'

'No.' Brit said it again, said it of Link.

'Think it over,' said Hilary. 'Perhaps you could make a business deal of it.'

'That's all it would be,' Brit came in quickly.

'You could offer Mr. Wayland an attractive profit,'

Hilary went on with it, ignoring Brit's interruption.

'I couldn't.'

'Think it over,' Hilary urged again.

Cara ... the old Cara once more ... tackled Brit that afternoon.

'Brit, I want to take over the reins of the boutique. I can make a go of it, a wonderful go of it. Brit, I *know* I can!'

'Yes, Cara, I've seen your talent,' Brit said a little wearily.

'You have to have a hard streak, Brit, and you haven't. You'd never make it prosper in a hundred years.'

'Perhaps, Cara, but money comes into it as well as talent, and I've told you all along that money is what I have *not* got.'

Now Cara said what Hilary had, only Cara said 'he', not 'Mr. Wayland.'

'He has it.'

'So?'

'So you're his wife. Look, Brit, I don't know what went wrong between you two, but I still think he's pretty abject to have left you high and dry like this.'

'He didn't. He doesn't know. He thinks I have plenty.' Brit stopped at the astounded look on Cara's face.

'You mean you pretended that——'

'Yes.'

Cara was dumbfounded. After a long pause all she could manage to say was—— 'Oh, Brit!' She recovered, though. She said triumphantly: 'Then I'll tell him.'

'Cara, you're not to. Cara, you mustn't!'

'I'll tell him, Brit. *If you don't go to him and offer him a profit in Simeon's if he will invest I'll tell Link.* Look' ... Cara took out papers ... 'I've written everything down. You might not understand the figures, but that tycoon will. It's my bet he'll invest very deeply.'

'He won't be asked to,' Brit insisted.

'He will, though. If you don't ask him, I shall. Then as I do it I'll tell him how you've been living from hand to mouth, not on the fat of the land as you let him think. You'll feel, and be, a complete fool, Brit.'

'No!'

'You have no choice.'

'No,' Brit repeated.

'Do I go—or you?' Cara asked warningly. 'I'm in dead earnest, Brit. Which of us? I mean that.'

Some time later ... Cara still waiting relentlessly by Brit's side ... Brit said miserably:

'I suppose I will.' She closed the subject by turning definitely away.

But when Cara had skipped triumphantly off, Brit sat on looking into space, looking wretchedly, dismally, futilely, dreading what lay ahead. What, she thought distastefully, can I say to Link? How long can I put the asking off?

However Cara was not one to let the grass grow. 'You must do it at once,' she said, coming in soon after to report a difficult but very lucrative sale. 'As a matter of fact, Brit, I took the liberty of ringing your husband, telling him you wanted a word with him.'

'Oh, Cara!'

'Well, it had to be personal, hadn't it? You could never hope to achieve anything over a phone.'

'You should have left it to me.'

'And never get it done! I told Link you had to see him, then asked where and when, and he said at his city hotel room would be the best, and to come around nine tonight.' Cara looked at Brit curiously. 'He didn't say which hotel ... would you know it?'

Would she know it? Brit sat for a very still moment remembering her wedding night ... Link holding her in his arms as she never had been held before, eyes to eyes, lips to lips. Breath-close. Thought-close. Link saying of John and Simeon: 'Ghosts. Dreams. I'm a man—your man.'

'Yes, I know it,' Brit said.

'Nine, then—Darling, put on one of our new dresses. —"Our" already! Brit had to smile.

But when Cara went out again, she did not smile. She was withdrawing with every fibre of her from the approaching interview. She was dreading Link's dark extracting eyes, Link's thinned lips.

She did not want a scene, recriminations, reproaches, explanations, appeals. What did she want? she thought dully. And then it came clearly, shiningly clearly, to her ... She wanted to hear Link saying as he had said that time in Hawaii, that bright dawn after that night in the Hawaiian inn:

'Good morning. Have a happy day.' Warm. Smiling. Both arms outstretched. The authentic Hawaiian greeting.

But could morning ever be good again? Could there be a happy day?

Cara opened the door. 'This dress, I think. And, Brit, for heaven's sake, *smile*!'

The hotel proprietor smiled at Brit as she came up to the desk.

'Nice to see you again, Mrs. Wayland. Mr. Wayland has been telling us how busy you've been, yet how successful. Well, your gain has been our loss. We've missed seeing you.' He turned and took down a key. 'The same room. Shall Harry take up your bags?'

'No bags,' Brit said. She went to the lift.

The seventh floor. She remembered watching the number in the indicator as the figures flashed on, then flashed off again. At the seventh the door opened and Brit went down the corridor to the suite of rooms right at the end. This was classified in the hotel list of accommodation as the honeymoon unit, or so Link once had told her. She put the key in the lock and went in.

She had half expected Link to be there, it would be one of those deliberately surprising things he would do. But the suite was empty. She took off her coat, put it on a chair, carefully kept her gaze from the large bed ... Link had insisted on a king-sized bed, had even had the hotel régime upset until one had been installed ... then she went and sat in her old position at the window. To wait.

How often had she waited here, very reluctant, all of her protesting, yet somewhere in that reluctance and that protestation ...

She looked down on the busy street far below. I wish it was another scene, she thought, I wish it was pink dawn in Hawaii and I was waking in a room fragrant with honeyed hibiscus and Link was smiling at me and saying:

'Good evening, Brit.' Link stood at the door.

She looked at him hungrily; she had not seen him for weeks. In case he saw the eagerness, immediately she turned her eyes away. He always had had a talent for knowing what she thought. He must not know now.

'You're thinner, Link.'

He came in casually, pulled out another chair and sat back to front in it, arms around the top rail. He faced Brit.

'Pining for you,' he proffered teasingly. When she did not respond, he said: 'Well, what's this all about?'

'Cara didn't tell you?'

'Only asked the time and the place. So your little sister is back?'

'Yes.'

'Thrown it in?'

'Well——'

'I hardly think she made the top in that short time.' His voice was laconic. 'Even,' he added, 'if your friend John did.'

'John went over practically assured of success.'

'And got it. Though why is he back here?'

'He's not—not now. He left at once,' Brit told him.

'Left at once?' Link stared at her. 'Yet you ... Oh, I see. You're following. But before you go, in dutiful sisterly fashion you want Cara settled. Oh, yes, Cara told me how much she liked the business. The pieces are falling into a pattern. The penny is dropping. How much do you want, Brit?'

'You've reached a wrong conclusion.'

'How much?' he repeated.

'Well, if you want it that way, here's the prospectus, or a prospectus I suppose you could call it.' Brit handed Link Cara's sheet of paper—What had Cara said? ... 'You might not understand the figures, but that tycoon will.'

He accepted the sheet and took his time scrutinizing it.

'I see.' He put in down.

'Well?'

'Promising. Quite promising.' A pause. 'But where do I come in?'

'I ... we thought you might like to invest,' faltered Brit.

'Is that necessary? I mean, with the money Simeon left you——'

'Simeon left me only the boutique, a very beautiful but unprofitable boutique. I think ... Hilary and the others think that Simeon hoped that someone with capital could save it.'

'Name of Wayland,' Link grinned, but it was a thin, unamused grin.

'Yes.'

There was silence for a while, then Link said:

'You really meant that about inheriting no money?'

'There wasn't a great deal. Simeon wasn't rich, but what he had to pass on went to his staff. They're a loyal and devoted staff.'

'I see. Then what have you been living on? You've never touched one of my cheques.'

'I'm alive.'

'Answer me, Brit!'

'I'm breathing, aren't I?' She said it a little apprehensively; she could see that old rage beginning to burn in his eyes.

'You were starving, but you wouldn't come to me.'

'Don't be melodramatic. I wasn't starving, I was simply having to make ends meet.'

'But you wouldn't come?'

'No.'

'How you must hate me.' He said it in an almost matter-of-fact voice, as though it was unimportant to him.

'And why the appeal now?' he asked presently. He was taking out his makings, and she realized how much she had missed that ritual.

'I'm giving the business to my sister,' she explained.

'Giving Cara her chance.'

'I think ... I feel sure ... it will be right this time, she has exceptional talent—also, surprisingly, she has a good business head.'

'Not like you.'

'No,' Brit agreed.

'That's very true. Cara would have taken all that offered.' Link was still spreading tobacco, rolling it up, thinning it again. 'She wouldn't have slummed it in some down-at-heel dump.'

'It's clean and respectable.'

'However,' he went on, 'perhaps I'm underrating your business acumen, perhaps the smaller things are discarded but the bigger issues carefully attended.'

'What do you mean?'

'I mean *John* could have settled Cara, he's in the big money now, he told me. But that big money is for you, I should say for both of you, so *I* am called upon for sister Cara. I'd like to say No, Brit, not on your life, Brit, but actually I can't. I'm responsible for you until we are legally separated, until you remarry, so I have to fork out whether I like it or not. So I will. How you use the cash once I pass it over is not my concern, but the law does expect me ostensibly to keep you.'

'I don't need your ostensible keep, I'm just offering you a favourable proposition.'

'It appears like that, but actually yours is a case of: "John can take care of me but not my sister as well, Wayland's my lawful husband, why should he get off scot free?"'

'You are,' said Brit in a low taut voice, 'a very cruel man.'

The tobacco was still in the large palm, the strong fingers were still flattening and rolling it.

'You should be the last to say that,' Link drawled. 'You've been afforded every material comfort. It's not my fault you've been on iron rations the last few weeks.'

'Cruelty comes in other forms,' she reminded him.

'You say cruel things.'
'Like?'
'Like believing I would do that. Go away with John, yet expect you to help me out with Cara.'
'Isn't it what you're doing?'
'I told you, Link, John has left.'
'And once you have Cara accounted for, you're following.'
'I am not following,' she insisted.
He was packing the tobacco into the paper now, putting the weed in neatly, tapping each end to get rid of any surplus shreds.
'Why?' he asked.
'I'm just not going.'
'He didn't ask you?'
'He asked me, but I'm not going. Link, *I am not going*. Can't you understand that?'
'No,' Link said. He waited a moment, then he reminded her: 'You loved the fellow. You never denied it.'
'There was nothing between us.'
'Yet you loved him.'
'I thought I did. When he came back——'
'You had had the taste of something better?'
'Must it always come back to money?' she sighed.
'I was not,' Link said, 'speaking of money.' His dark eyes flicked narrowly at her, and once more she remembered fierce arms around her, a voice saying: 'Ghosts. Dreams. I am your man.'
His tongue was darting out to lick the paper edges together, and she turned away.
'You never liked that, did you?' There was banter in Link's lazy voice.
'You notice things,' she commented.
'I've noticed them ever since I first saw you, Brit,

and decided what was to be done.'

She had heard that story before, but never the reason behind it.

'Why was it to be me?' she asked.

'You stood there a little behind the family group. Remember, Brit, I'd come to interview your father. I saw you like I knew I'd been—lonely, not wanted, hungry.'

'I wasn't!' she said indignantly.

'Oh, yes, you were, don't you think I know the symptoms? I've had them all myself. I did have a good granny, but she died, and that made it all the worse. But you had no one, you poor little mutt.'

'So it was pity?'

'Oh, no' ... firmly ... 'it was never pity. If it had been that I needn't have gone through the ritual, need I? Marriage and the rest.'

'Then it was——' But she could not finish. How could she ask this hard man if, apart from physical satisfaction, she had ever meant anything to him, anything at all?

'Finish it, Brit,' he drawled.

'It would be a waste of time, Link. I've only ever been a possession to you, something you put money out on, so naturally couldn't let go.'

'You think that, do you?'

'What else can I think? Have you ever given me any real tenderness? Have you ever said that you love me?'

'And have it thrown back at me, if not in actual words, then in John, in Simeon?'

'I've told you and told you,' she said in despair.

'But you haven't told me what you want me to tell you. Be fair, Brit. You have to come half way as well.'

She said simply: 'I love you.' She waited for his reaction.

It was disappointing. 'Interesting,' he said. 'And when did this remarkable state of affairs first occur to you?'

'I think it was in that Hawaiian hotel, the first inn I ever saw with a fountain singing out of a big shell. You woke me up' ... she knew her cheeks were burning ... 'and said: "Good morning. Have a happy day."'

'Which you proceeded to have soon after with Simeon.'

'Link!' She almost shouted it. 'Link, do you have to go on like this?'

'Yes, because I'm tired of being hurt, Brit, I'm tired of giving and not receiving, of kissing and not being the kissed. It would be pleasant to believe you, pleasant to have all this over, but I'm still not sure, what's more I'm not even sure if you're worth it, girl.'

'What do you want me to do?' she half-cried. When he did not answer, she said: 'Because I'll do it, Link.'

He stood up.

'I'm going out. I'm going to walk the city. No' ... as she went to rise as well ... 'you're not coming, too. Go to bed, Brit. Or sit here and look out. But don't try to follow me. I have to find myself. Know myself. I've been a roughrider ... oh, yes, you were right. I believed I had only to ride hard and long and the world was mine.'

'It is yours,' she said eagerly, 'and you weren't a roughrider.'

'I was, and I got what I went after. But now I don't know if I want it ... either that, or maybe it's come too late.'

'No, Link,' she appealed. She put out her hand, but he turned away.

'I want to know myself,' he said again.

'Then know me, too,' she pleaded ... but she called only to the door.

She heard his footsteps along the passage. She heard the lift descending. Then there was nothing, nothing for hours, for Brit sat on there for all those hours, sat on so long that dawn came in, a rather yellow dawn, the dawns big cities put on, the sun rays mixed with dust and grey-tinged with commerce. Oh, for a pink Hawaiian break of day!

Then she heard the lift. The steps. The turning of the door handle. He had come to say ... oh, what had he come to say?

He stood there a long, long moment looking at her, and all at once she recognized in the look as well as a possession, a pride, an authority, a mastery—for Link would always have these; they were Link—a very tender love.

When he came to her, Brit knew intrinsically, as well as passion there would be a great gentleness. A lover's gentleness. She waited for that ... and for him.

And across the room he saw her waiting, and he outstretched both arms as he said with a promise as well as a greeting:

'Good morning, Mrs. Wayland. Have a happy day.'

THE OMNIBUS

Has Arrived!

A GREAT NEW IDEA

From HARLEQUIN